MISDIRECTED

A NOVEL

ALI BERMAN

Seven Stories Press
Triangle Square books for young readers
NEW YORK • OAKLAND

Seven Stories Press
140 Watts Street
New York, NY 10013
www.sevenstories.com

College professors and high school and middle school teachers may order free examination copies of Seven Stories Press titles. To order, visit www.sevenstories.com/contact or send a fax on school letterhead to (212) 226-1411.

Book design by Jon Gilbert

Library of Congress Cataloging-in-Publication Data

Berman, Ali.
  Misdirected : a novel / by Ali Berman.
    pages cm
  Summary: When fifteen-year-old Ben moves to small-town Colorado and a Christian school, his atheism sets him apart and leads to bullying and misunderstandings, and with his brother serving in Iraq and his sister away at college Ben is on his own in the struggle to find his place without compromising who he is.
  ISBN 978-1-60980-573-9 (hardback)
  [1. Conduct of life--Fiction. 2. Faith--Fiction. 3. Bullies--Fiction. 4. High schools--Fiction. 5. Schools--Fiction. 6. Magic tricks--Fiction. 7. Moving, Household--Fiction.] I. Title.
  PZ7.B45355Mis 2014
  [Fic]--dc23
                                    2014010183

Printed in the United States

9 8 7 6 5 4 3 2 1

For David and Glenda Berman
(the best parents ever).

Chapter 1

BECAUSE YOUR PARENTS SAID SO

live in Massachusetts, about thirty minutes outside of
Boston. I'm a Bay Stater. Or a suburban Bostonian. A
New Englander.

Yep, I can still say that. I wouldn't even care if people
called me a masshole, if it meant I could stay here.

My parents told me a month ago that we're moving.
My mom got a new job, better pay and all the things
adults care about. What don't they care about? Taking
me out of high school the week before my sophomore
year and moving me three quarters of the way across
the country to a crap town in Colorado called Forest
Ridge.

My dad works from home so it doesn't matter to
him where we go. Being a middle-aged man without an
office job, it's not like he has any friends anyway.

They say that I'm not seeing it from their perspective.
I say, if they could remember how hard high school is,
they'd never ask me to move. But they're old. So there
it is. We're going.

My mom said, "At least you haven't started dating

yet. Imagine how much harder it would be if you had to leave a girlfriend behind."

Thanks, Mom. Really. Thanks for the reminder that I'm fifteen and haven't even kissed a girl. It makes me feel so good to have that fact pointed out by you. Not that I'm so unusual. Most of my friends have yet to make contact. Probably because they (okay, we) aren't the coolest bunch.

Well, Seth has. Or so he says. He claims it happened at summer camp when he was thirteen. But with summer camp stories, there is always the very real chance that they are total bull. If I had gone to summer camp, I'd have probably had a fake girlfriend too.

I guess I sort of kissed a girl. If we're being technical. Seth and I hang out with this girl Margaret Fong. She's not really the person I want to remember being my first kiss. She's more best-friend material than the girl you imagine making out with. It was in eighth grade, on a dare, and we didn't use tongue. Even though it was on the mouth it only lasted about as long as I would kiss my dog. Not that she's a dog. I mean, I like Margaret. She's even decent looking. I just don't like her like that. Seth brings it up once in a while to embarrass us both.

Man, I'm going to miss those guys.

Seth and Margaret come over a few minutes before we're supposed to leave for the airport. Usually we'd all go up to my room, but it's empty now. My stuff is on a truck on some big long highway. The only things left are the stickers of the solar system I put up on my ceiling ten years ago during my planets-are-cool phase. And they've lost their glow anyway. Plus, it's not even accurate anymore. Not since Pluto got tossed.

We go outside and sit in the backyard. Seth hands me

something wrapped in newspaper. A gift. It's a book on magic.

Now I know what you're thinking. Magic is kind of lame when you're past birthday parties for six-year-olds. But I do awesome magic. The kind that gets people to ask you afterward, "How the hell did you do that?" And I say, like a bit of a jerk, "Magic."

Last year I got beat up because I wouldn't tell this big kid how to do an illusion. We were in the lunchroom, and I was semi-successfully impressing two girls with some easy card manipulation, when he came over and demanded step-by-step instructions on how to pull it off. I told him to shove it. He responded by punching me in the eye socket and shouting, "Magically fix that, asshole!"

Turns out my older sister, Emily, had a bit of illusion-worthy makeup in her bag. She slopped some beige goo below my eye and you could hardly tell it was all blackened underneath. I wore a hat and looked at people from my right side for a few days and no one noticed. Although my mom kept telling me, "Sweetie, you look so tired."

Now Emily is in college down in New York. Last week, when she left, I gave her a sappy Belle and Sebastian CD and she gave me a bottle of concealer labeled "wuss cream."

Seth doesn't care about magic at all. He likes baseball and soccer and other sports that require hitting, kicking, and chasing things. On the other hand, Margaret is really good at it. Better than me, mostly because she's been doing it longer. Unlike me, she won't do it in front of people she doesn't know well. So her audience consists of me, Seth, her mom, and little brother.

I swear she could fool Houdini, but no one will ever know because she's too goddamn scared. Plus, she can do the tricks in English and Cantonese, which just ups the coolness factor.

I think high school is going to get harder for them without me here. Then again, they still have it easier than me. I'm going to a brand new school where I have *no* friends.

Seth says, pointing to the book, "I don't know if you have this one, but it looked pretty cool."

"I don't. Thanks, man."

"Sure."

We're silent and awkward for a minute while I flip through the book.

"I've never seen some of these," I say, mostly lying. There is one toward the back I don't have.

Seth gives a half-embarrassed nod. I don't think he's ever given me something before. Even on birthdays, we'd usually just sneak into an R-rated movie.

Margaret takes a small wrapped rectangle out of her bag. Not a book. Something about the size of her . . . Holy crap. Is that . . .

"Is that your McBride collection?"

"Normally a person opens something before they find out what it is."

I grab it and rip off the paper. It is. It's her DVD set of Jeff McBride videos that she's been learning from for years. The man is the master of cards.

"You can't give me this. It's like giving away your mentor."

"You need it more than me, right? I've memorized the DVDs so it's your turn now."

I sit there for a minute looking down at McBride's

face and then stand up and give her the biggest hug I know how to give.

Seth says right on cue, "Dude, no kissing. I'm right here."

And he's right. The hug goes on a little longer than I expected it to. Just long enough to be slightly weird as we let go. I don't want to kiss her exactly, although her skin has cleared up since that dare back in middle school. I am going to miss her. I probably could have hugged her for another five minutes, if Seth wasn't staring at us. Sometimes I think he likes Margaret. Not that he would ever admit it.

I sit back down and stare at both of them. Right now, Seth and Margaret look kind of like my dog Holly when she watched my brother Pete leave for his first tour in Iraq. Or like she did last week, when my sister went off to Sarah Lawrence after packing half her room into the car. They look like they're being abandoned.

"You think your parents will let you visit?" I ask them.

Margaret says, "Visiting a boy all the way out in Colorado? Not likely."

"I'm not a boy. I'm Ben. It's totally different."

"We'll see," she says.

"What about you?" I ask Seth.

"I dunno. Depends on my grades."

"Maybe you should do your homework for once."

"Homework sucks."

"Without me here, what else are you going to do at night?"

He punches me in the calf in the exact place where the muscle feels like it's got an edge. He might not be that great at math, but he has a good enough understanding of the human body to hit exactly where it will hurt the most.

"At least now you'll have less competition for Diane Schwartz," I say.

Margaret rolls her eyes.

"Like you were competition," he says.

"She would have come around. As girls get older they care less about tall and muscular and more about, you know, other things."

"Pale and skinny?" asks Margaret with a grin, as she flips through the book Seth gave me.

My mom pokes her head out the door and calls to me.

"Sweetie, we've got to get going. Oh, hi, Seth. Hi, Margaret."

"Hi, Mrs. Pinter," they say in unison.

My mom waves to me one more time and then heads back out front. I put the book and the DVDs in my backpack along with my other stuff that will keep me occupied on the plane.

"Well."

"Yeah," Seth says.

"Wish me luck."

"Wish you luck? How about us?" asks Seth.

"You don't need luck. You just need to talk to more people."

"I don't like people."

"Just invite them over to kick a ball around or something. And you," I say, looking at Margaret, "get up the nerve to do your magic in public. You're too good to keep performing for your stuffed animals. And, seriously, way too old."

"Shut up," she says, smiling before giving me a weird

sort of half hug. I guess that last full hug was so strange that she can't give me another one. Too much confusing male/female body parts touching, even though we're just friends, so it shouldn't matter, but it does.

"We'll be visiting my sister over Thanksgiving. My mom already promised, so I'll see you. Sarah Lawrence is only a few hours away."

"Yeah, okay," says Seth.

"I've got to go."

"Good luck, man," he says.

"You too."

Seth and Margaret turn and walk through the backyard and into the woods that connects to the path back to his house. I stand there and wait for them to turn around. They don't. I can see them laughing and talking. So, by myself, I head out to the front of the house that is no longer my house and get in the back of the car with Holly. She looks happy that we're taking her with us and not leaving her, like Pete and Emily did. So why do I feel like I'm the one being left behind now?

Chapter 2

MAGIC IS NOT FOR LOSERS

t's Saturday morning in the new house. Every room is filled with boxes.

Even though he's not here, hasn't been here in months, and won't be back for many more months, my mom unpacks Pete's room first. She turns it into a replica of his room back home. In fact, when it came to picking rooms, she chose the one that looked the most like his old room. It's also the biggest.

Back in Mass, I helped her pack up Pete's room and had a really awkward moment when she found some magazines under his mattress.

"Think I should put these in a care package?" she asked.

"Um. I think he's probably set," I said, trying not to stare at the girl on the cover.

When she unpacks his stuff in the new room, she even puts those "nighttime magazines"—that's what she called them—back under his mattress. Seriously.

I guess that's okay. We all miss Pete. But my mom misses him on a whole other level. It's a good thing his tour ends soon. He'll meet us in the new house in December. Mom wants his room to be comfortable for him.

Meanwhile, I can't find a damn thing in this new house. Even though I look everywhere, I can't find my magic stuff. School starts on Monday and I have no friends. I'd like to fix that before I show up and have zero people to sit with at lunch. Mark, this transfer student kid back home, told me that sitting alone when you're new turns you into a big social black hole. Making even one friend before school starts will make me way less loser-y. Doing magic is the only icebreaker I know.

I take Margaret's DVDs out of my bag and put them next to the bed. Without knowing which box my supplies are in, I grab a coin and some paper for the disappearing coin trick. It's not flashy but it's a crowd pleaser. I put on my *I'm cool enough to talk to even though I'm doing magic tricks* clothes and head outside.

Sure, I should be helping my parents unpack an entire house full of stuff, but making friends seems way more important right now.

At my old school, I was smart enough to get better grades than most kids, but not athletic enough to be popular. At my age, people want you to be good at everything. Math, science, art, English, football, baseball. From the age of five right through eighteen, we need to be renaissance kids. As soon as we show that we're bad at something, you can almost hear the grown-ups thinking, *Well, I guess he'll never be an Olympic athlete or a neurosurgeon* or whatever else we suck at.

Notice I didn't put magic on that list of talents people care about. It's because they don't.

The new house is on a street with a bunch of other similar houses. Kind of 1970s. The neighborhood is clean, near the two-street-light town, and there are basketball hoops in front of a few houses. There are lots of SUVs and trucks in driveways. And that means that families live here.

There are no kids outside yet. It's only 10 a.m. so I set up. I even have a back-up card trick in case anything goes wrong with the coin.

I hang out for a while and practice my fanning. A few cars drive by. They wave but they don't stop.

A girl in the house across the street, about my age, looks out the window. I smile and hold up the coin dramatically and mouth the word, "magic?"

She smiles back and disappears. She's gone for so long that I think she only smiled to be polite or she had no idea what I said.

A few minutes later the door opens and she walks out with an older girl and two younger boys.

The girl from the window walks right up to me, holds out her hand, and says, "I'm Tess. This is my sister Angela. And these are my little brothers, Dan and Paul."

Tess is cute, but her sister Angela is downright hot.

"I'm Ben," I say. "We just moved in yesterday."

"Welcome," says Tess. "Are you going to Christian Heritage Academy?"

"I am, yeah. I'll be a sophomore."

"Me too!" she says. "Angela's going to be a senior. And these two are in third and fourth grade."

Angela nods but she looks kind of bored. I must

entertain. So I say to one of the kids, "Do you like magic?"

He nods his head as fast as he can.

"Do any of you have a coin?" I ask. "A nickel or a quarter would be perfect."

Tess takes a quarter out of her jean shorts pocket. She might not be as good- looking as her sister, but she's as nice as nice gets. She's smiling encouragingly at me, kind of like someone's mom would. Like someone who genuinely wants to like you. It's a little weird, but way better than Angela who alternates between picking at her nails and looking back toward her house.

The kids are into it though, so I take Tess's coin and start the trick by folding the coin into the paper. While folding, I press it against my hand, fast enough so that it just looks like part of the fold. When the coin disappears, the outline of the coin on the paper will make it look like it's still there. This is the first illusion I learned back when my brother took me to my first magic show. I hung around at the end for so long that the magician, back in his street clothes, showed me how to do it. Pete helped me practice for a week until no one could see the coin drop into my pocket.

And now I do it again, like I've done hundreds of times. The coin is gone.

The kids all clap. So does Tess. Angela gives a few half smacks against her jeans with one hand. In her other hand is her phone. She was texting. So she's good- looking and totally rude.

Dan says, "You should do that at our church talent show. What church is your family going to?"

"Oh. We don't actually go to church."

"Why not?" he asks.

"We're not really religious."

Dan is silent. Angela looks up from her phone. Paul is still focused on the paper in my hand so I pass it to him. Tess smiles at me, but she looks kind of worried.

"Are you Jewish?" Angela asks.

"No. We're not really anything."

"So you're an atheist," she says accusingly.

"I guess, I don't know."

"Why are you going to a Christian school?"

"My parents want me to go to a private school and it's the only one in town. I went to a Catholic school back home."

Dan looks up. He's holding the ripped up pieces of paper.

"What's an atheist?"

Angela says, "It's nothing, Danny. Come on. Let's get back home. Mom has snacks out."

The two younger kids follow Angela back home. They smile and wave as they cross the street. I wave back. Tess stands in front of me.

"What did I say wrong?" I asked.

"Our older brother is an atheist. Our mom and dad don't talk to him anymore. They don't let us talk to him either."

"Did he do something?"

She laughs. "Yeah, he became an atheist."

"What's wrong with that?"

"Where are you from?" she asks.

"Just outside of Boston. We have Christians there. And Jews and Muslims and Buddhists and lots of other people who just aren't into religion."

"We don't really have atheists here. And if we did,

people wouldn't talk to them unless they were trying to convert them."

"So did I just freak your sister out?"

"Pretty much. In fact, she's probably telling her friends about you right now."

"Okay, so maybe I'll try to avoid the topic of religion if it comes up?"

"Oh Ben," she says, shaking her head a little and laughing. "You can't avoid that topic here."

I look at her, confused.

"Tell you what. Sit with me at lunch on Monday. I'll help you through it."

"You're kind of freaking me out."

"You have no idea," she says as she starts to walk away. She turns back and says, "Thanks for the trick. The coin went in your pocket, right?"

"You saw?"

"No, you did it really well. It's just that that's the only time you could have switched it. Anyway, see you at school."

Chapter 3

SISTERS KISS GIRLS TOO

Going to a religious school isn't going to be totally out of the ordinary. I'm used to ignoring the morning prayers and the annoying buzz of the teacher's voice in theology class (which should really just be called Jesus class since that's the only theology we ever talked about). My mom and dad actually thought about switching me to public school in Forest Ridge, but the private school had a much better reputation, even if they said it was a bit more devout.

Not all the kids were Christian at my old school. I mean, Seth is Jewish. Margaret is kind of a half-assed Buddhist. And even the kids who were really into Jesus didn't always go to church on Sundays.

That night at dinner, we're sitting at the table eating pizza. Usually my dad cooks, but they are still unpacking all the kitchen stuff.

"Are we atheists?" I ask suddenly.

Mom and Dad look up, their mouths hanging open a bit.

Dad recovers first and says, "Well, we're not a religious family."

"But are we atheists? I mean, I've never really thought about it."

"We aren't any one thing as a family," Mom says. "Each of us is free to believe whatever we want."

"So, what are you guys?"

"Well," Dad says, "I do not believe in god."

"I believe there might be something," says Mom, "I don't believe anyone knows what it is. There are just lots of different interpretations out there."

"I met some kids across the street," I say. "They didn't seem too happy when I said we weren't religious and that I don't really believe in god."

"Why did that come up?" asks Dad.

"They asked me what church we were going to and I said, *none*. Then they asked if we were atheists."

They look at each other briefly and then Mom says, "You might find Forest Ridge to be a little more religious than you're used to back home."

"How much more religious?"

"Just remember that it's important to respect other people's beliefs," she says. "Do that and you'll be just fine."

"Yeah, of course. It's just, well, maybe we should have looked into public school."

"You never minded your private school back in Massachusetts. Besides, you're used to a religious school. It provides good structure," she says.

"But we're not religious. And back at my last school, nobody cared."

"Doesn't matter. Whether we're religious or not, the moral foundations are the same."

"I'm not sure they're exactly the same. I mean, *Don't kill people* and *Don't rob people* might be the same. Other stuff is different."

"Well, you've got independent thought. Use it," she says with a smile.

Dad slops two more pieces of pizza onto his plate and changes the subject.

"Ben, have you heard from Emily at all?"

"She texted me this morning wishing me luck with the new school."

"Well, she won't answer her phone. Can you try calling her tonight? Just to make sure she's okay."

"She started college, like, a week ago. She's busy."

"Just call her and say hello."

"Yeah. Okay."

After dinner, with a few pieces of pizza crust in my pocket, I take Holly for a walk around the block. I look over at Tess's house. The light is on, and they are doing the same thing we just did. Eating dinner as a family. With Pete and Emily gone, I'm now the only kid to talk to during dinner. Em used to fill up a lot of that space.

She would talk about college and how she couldn't wait to get to school and study and live in New York City. Not that she didn't love Boston, but New York City, besides being home to the suckalicious Yankees, has a lot more going on.

She likes books and can't wait to go to readings and museums and do all that boring stuff. She better not make me do that crap when I go visit her.

I don't even really know what kids do when they get to college. I guess drinking is a big thing. I haven't had anything other than a sip of my dad's beer yet. Maybe when I go visit my sister she'll let me try stuff.

I take out my phone and call her.

"Hey, Sis."

"Hey."

"Why aren't you answering Mom and Dad's phone calls?"

"I'm fine, thanks. How are you?"

"No, really. They're worried."

"They shouldn't be. I'm fine."

"Then tell them that."

"I did already. I emailed them."

"Email isn't good enough. Just call them."

"I'm not ready to."

"Why the hell not?"

"Because."

"Because what?"

"I'm just dealing with choosing classes and stuff," she says, somewhat cryptically.

"Maybe they could help."

"Just tell them that I'm fine."

"How much does your school cost a semester? Seriously, you call them and tell them you're fine."

"Just give me some time. I'll call when I'm ready."

"Time for what?"

She sighs on the other end of the line and there is a bit of a pause.

"You can't tell them," she says, finally.

"Tell them what?"

"Look, I'm about to tell you something major. Are you near Mom or Dad?"

"No. I'm outside with Holly. Are you okay?"

"I'm fine. It's not like that. It's just something that's going to be surprising."

"Just tell me."

There is a long pause. Like, thirty seconds. I feel like I'm playing chicken. Who will speak first?

Finally, Em says, "I think I'm gay."

It takes me a solid ten seconds to register what she just said. "Gay? As in, you're into girls?" I say, finally.

"No, gay as in happy. Yes, you idiot. Into girls."

"You think? Or you know?"

"I know."

Before my mind has time to wrap around the new information I spit out the first thing I think of.

"You went out with Tony Macalister, like six months ago."

"For a week. He was gross."

"Are you sure you don't like all guys? Maybe it's just gross guys like Tony."

"Are you seriously going to ask me ignorant ass questions like that?"

"Sorry. I just . . . it's kind of weird. Are you dating someone?"

"Yeah. My roommate."

"You can't date your roommate!"

"Why not?"

"Because it's not dating. You're living together. It's going from zero to five thousand in like two-point-five seconds."

"You can't tell Mom and Dad."

"Damn right I can't. You have to."

"I can't. Not yet. I've been gone a week and then I'm going to call them up and say I'm gay?"

"Well, maybe you don't have to tell them right away. You can at least call them to say that you're okay and that college is good."

"What do I say? I don't want to lie."

"You don't have to lie. When they ask, *How are you getting along with your roommate?* You can just say, *So much better than I expected!*"

"Oh shut up."

"Anyway, Mom and Dad aren't going to care if you're gay."

"They'll think it's a phase."

"So what? In ten years when you're still gay, you'll have proven them wrong."

"Thanks," she says. "And thanks for not freaking out."

"You mean, freak out that my sister is kissing girls before I am? That's an issue for my ego."

"Maybe girls would kiss you if you weren't such a sarcastic turd."

"Thanks, Em. So how long have you known?"

"For a while now. But there were no other gay kids in our school, so it didn't seem like a good time to be unique. This place is like queer-girl heaven."

"Maybe there were other gay kids, but everyone was like you, too scared to say anything. Anyway, it's Massachusetts. We have gay marriage."

"Think I really wanted to hear dyke jokes from the entire male population at school? They couldn't even handle me being vegan."

"Yeah. Maybe I'm giving too much credit to the kids at our old school."

"So are you excited for your new school?" she asks, changing the subject.

"How many ways can I say no?"

"Why not? Brand new place. You can be as awesome as you want to be."

"It seems kind of Christian."

"Well, you're used to that."

"Yeah. We'll see."

"Okay. Well, text me and let me know how it goes."

"Only if you call Mom and Dad and tell them you're good and having fun and learning stuff."

"Classes haven't even started yet."

"Call anyway."

"Fine, I will."

"Hey, sis."

"Yeah?"

"Are you an atheist?"

"Where is that question coming from? What, gay people can't believe in god?"

"No. I'm just asking if you do or if you don't."

"I don't believe."

"Me neither," I say. "Do you think it matters?"

"Matters to who?"

"Other people."

"It shouldn't matter, right? I mean, who cares what you believe or who you love as long as you're a good person."

"Yeah."

"Okay, I'm going to call Mom and Dad."

"Later, Sis."

"Later, Bro."

Chapter 4

LYING IS APPARENTLY A GODLY THING TO DO

The first day in a new school pretty much sucks no matter what. All the kids are a combination of excited about seeing their old friends and nervous about the school year. No one is really interested in making a new friend. They're too busy seeing who got taller, who grew boobs, and who got their braces off.

At least, that's what would have happened at my old school. In this place, about ten kids come right up to me and introduce themselves before classes even start. Nine out of ten of them ask me what church I'll be attending. I shake off the question by saying, "Oh, I'm not sure yet."

I was able to throw most of them off the scent but this group of guys, Kenny, Stan, and Arty, asked me if I wanted to try out their church. And I said, "Sure. Thanks!" putting on my best *Jesus is great* face. I figure it's a good idea not to totally alienate myself. Church is boring but if that's what people are into here, then maybe I can suck it up. On the upside I have plans for the weekend.

Wow. My big weekend plans have become church. Back home I'd have had a movie marathon with Seth and Margaret.

I choose a seat in the back of class for homeroom. We go through the normal routine. We say the Pledge of Allegiance. I stop speaking when the "under god" part comes around. We talk about rules. They go through the morning prayer. I sort of mumble my way through it all, pretending. If I went to a public school, I wouldn't have to pretend. I'd get to go about my day without having to grovel in thanks every five minutes. I mean, my mom and dad gave me life. I don't high five them every half hour for that.

As I go from class to class, I start noticing all the differences between my old school and this one. School uniforms are required in both. In Massachusetts a bunch of the girls would roll their skirts up to show as much leg as possible without getting in trouble. Here, still skirts but no extra leg. Kind of a bummer. Also, I haven't heard a single curse word. Instead of saying, *Oh my god*, they say *Oh my gosh*. And *dang* instead of *damn*. Thinking on it, I say *goddamn, Jesus Christ*, and *oh my god* all the time.

By lunchtime, things change. People stop coming up to me to say hi. In fact, people are now looking at me as if I'm kind of weird. Angela sits a few tables over and when I wave hello, she gives a little wave back, and then proceeds to talk to her friends with great enthusiasm. Each of them turns to look back at me. Although they try to be sneaky about it, they totally fail.

Tess keeps her promise. She sees me sitting alone in the cafeteria, and instead of joining the group of friends waiting for her, she waves them off and takes a seat next to me.

"How is your first day going?"

"Not too bad. Everyone was oddly nice."

"Was?"

"Well, this morning people seemed really into meeting me. Now people are just kind of looking at me strangely."

"That's because everyone in school knows you're an atheist by now."

"How?!"

"My big-mouthed sister."

"Isn't gossip a sin or something?"

"Just because something is a sin doesn't mean people don't do it."

"Great," I say, sarcastically. "Well, I'm going to church with Kenny, Stan and Arty on Sunday. Maybe that will make people think I'm less sketchy."

"That's the church almost all of us go to. It's going to be different than what you're used to."

"I went to a Catholic school, remember?"

"People here pretty much think Catholics are full of it."

"What's the difference? They all believe in Jesus."

"There is a big difference."

I'm not a big fan of how she's talking to me. Like there's a joke I'm not in on and she's just waiting to laugh at me. Maybe she feels my frustration, because then she says quickly, "So what's your family like? What are you into?"

"I've got an older sister at Sarah Lawrence College and an older brother stationed in Iraq."

"You like magic," she adds.

"Can't get enough of it. Would do it all day if I could."

"Leave a girlfriend back home?" she asks point-blank.

"Just friends who are girls," I say, smiling and a little embarrassed.

"Why are you an atheist?"

"Why are you religious?"

"How do you know I am?"

"Because your family seems to like you and you told me they don't talk to your brother because he isn't religious."

"I could be faking."

"Are you?"

"No, but I don't believe a lot of the same stuff as my family and friends."

"You're Christian?"

"Of course."

"Well, that's not an *of course*. There are lots of religions a person could be."

"Not around here," she mutters.

"And by the way, I don't go around calling myself an atheist. It's not like this big label I wear. It's not important."

"It's important here."

"All the more reason for me not to call myself one, right?"

"Are you ashamed of it?"

I think for a minute and then say, "My grandma was Hungarian."

"What?" says Tess, looking at me strangely.

"On my dad's side, I'm Hungarian. I don't go around telling people I'm Hungarian. That doesn't mean I'm ashamed, does it?"

"Point taken."

Tess looks at me with her head kind of turned, like she's thinking about something but she's not sure she wants to tell me. "Is it ever scary?" she asks, finally.

"What?"

"Being out there alone. I mean, I'm never alone. It's impossible for me to be alone. But you, if you don't believe in God, then no one is watching out for you."

"My parents and my brother and sister and my friends back home. They care."

"They don't know your every thought. They didn't create you."

"I find it more comforting that my parents don't know my every thought. As for creating me, my fifth grade Sex Ed class says that they did."

Tess's face goes red. "That's not what I meant," she says, smiling.

She takes out a sandwich and some carrot sticks. She offers me some and I grab a few carrots and dip them in the extra peanut butter globbed on my sandwich.

"That's gross," she says.

"Try it."

She takes a carrot and rubs it across the bread and eats it.

"Not bad actually."

She takes a few more bites and asks me about Boston, about Catholic school and about magic. She talks a lot more than I'm used to. Even Margaret usually just listened to Seth and me BS most of the time.

I can't really figure out if Tess is just being nice or if she's flirting with me. I'm not even really sure what I would do if she were flirting. How does a guy flirt back?

Wow. I'm pretty sure asking that question makes me pathetic.

Before I have time to figure out what's happening, a cute girl with huge, curly, red hair walks over, stands a few feet away and points to her watch. Tess waves for her to come closer.

"Beth, this is Ben. He's new here."

"Hi," I say.

"Nice to meet you," she says. "Tess, I need to talk to you."

Tess looks at me.

"It's cool," I say. "I'll look for you later."

"I bet you will," Tess says, laughing. But it wasn't a flirty laugh. It sounded more like a *you're royally screwed and you don't even know it yet* kind of laugh.

Tess and Beth walk away whispering to each other. When they get about fifteen feet from my table, Beth looks back at me and giggles. I'm pretty sure it's a bad sign when girls just look at you and laugh.

I sit in the cafeteria for the rest of the lunch period by myself. If I were at my old school, Seth and Margaret and I would all be trading food and laughing about some stupid thing that happened the night before. I wouldn't be alone watching everyone stare at me. I'd have friends. Plural.

I go through the next few periods smiling at everyone who looks at me to show that I'm not Satan. By the end of the day my face hurts. Now that I've got a plan to go to church with the guys on Sunday, I have an answer to the inevitable church question, and maybe people will stop looking at me and whispering. I've met a lot of people, but the only real conversation I've had is with Tess.

The last period of the day is a welcome assembly. The teacher doesn't even say what it's for. She just tells us to go to the auditorium. I sit toward the back in an empty row of seats. Nearly everyone else is as close to the stage as they can get. All except me and one other kid who sits in the row behind me and a few seats to the left. I feel him looking at me. He doesn't say anything so I ignore him.

This guy in jeans and a button-down shirt goes on stage with a microphone and all the students cheer. Clapping, whooping, big loud cheering.

"Welcome back Christian Heritage Academy!"

A louder cheer blasts from every mouth around me. It's like a pep rally, only there's no football team.

"For those of you who don't know, I'm Frank Howard, your school voice to spread the word of our Lord Jesus Christ. I hope you all had a great summer. I heard some of you were counselors at your church Bible camps. Good for you. Helping spread the word to younger kids and setting a good example. Seriously, clap for yourselves!"

The students clap again, and I can't help but think that kids in my town would be laughed at for going to church camp. I always thought that was kind of stupid, making fun of kids just for going to camp, but clapping like it's the coolest thing in the world makes me laugh a little. This Frank guy looks at me, smiles, and carries on.

"Today, I want to talk about the summer, and about something all of us faced. Temptation. The desire to do bad things even though we know those things go against the teachings of Jesus Christ. Who here has been tempted? That's it. Raise your hands."

Hands go up everywhere. Even Frank's hand goes in the air.

"If you didn't raise your hand, you're lying. That's right. All of us face temptation. And sometimes we fail. We choose the wrong thing. We're human. Not a single one of us is righteous. Now, I'm guessing that all of you, yes I said all, have sinned during your time away this summer. You may not do it in front of your parents, or your friends, but when you turn your eye inward, and look at yourself, you know. You don't have to tell me about it. You know. And God knows. Whether it's indulging in lustful thoughts, greed, swearing, or any other sin, God knows what you did. And you know what? He loves you anyway. He knows that humanity is diseased and He died so that we might rise from our sins and be saved. Now, was anyone here saved this summer?"

A few hands go up.

"That's right!" he says to those hands. "You may fail sometimes, but now that you're saved, God is here to catch you. Anyone want to come up and tell us about it?"

A girl toward the back stands and approaches the stage. The other students cheer her on. I think I'm the only person in the room who has no idea what's going on. *Saved?*

The girl walks up to Frank and he hands her the microphone.

"Hey everyone. For my entire life I've wanted to feel the Holy Spirit and be saved. All of my friends had gone through it and I could tell my family was getting nervous that it hadn't happened yet. I loved church, but I had questions and doubts. That was until July when my family and I went to church and the preacher was speaking words that felt like they were coming from

God himself. I opened myself and let the words in and then it happened. I found Him."

Students all around stand up and cheer.

"It felt like I was connected to the world, to Jesus and all the reasons He died to save us. All my doubts were gone. I just felt so thankful. I thought my heart was going to explode. And I knew the Holy Spirit had come to me."

She smiles while the other students continue to cheer, and hands the microphone back to Frank.

"Thank you, Laura," says Frank. "That's what I'm talking about, people. Letting Christ's love into your heart. You can't just expect it to show up. If you have a party and don't invite anyone, do you think anyone is going to come? No! You have to send the invitations, ask people to visit. Same with Christ. He needs to know you're ready for Him. That you know He died so that you might be saved and then, only then, will you feel the wondrous feeling that Laura described. Only then will you truly be saved. Let's all pray to God that those of us who may not have been saved yet will be able to open themselves to the Holy Spirit soon."

I'll admit, at this point, I'm freaking out. I want to raise my hand and ask, *What the hell does getting saved mean?* But that would point out that I don't fit in here at all. I have that awful feeling in my stomach, like when you're at a party and no one talks to you. As Emily would say, *it's like being the only vegan at a pig roast.*

Frank talks for a while more about being saved and about the importance of loving Jesus. I clap when other people clap, but all I want to do is go home. Catholic school was nothing like this. Kids there barely talked about god.

"Now a bit of housekeeping," says Frank. "I want us to do some brainstorming. It's day one and everyone is excited to be here with their friends. It would be so easy to go about our daily lives, enjoying all that we have. Of course, we have to recognize that not everyone has all the joy we have. Not everyone is as fortunate as we are. That's right. It's time to start throwing out ideas for our fall service projects. Let's help people and spread the word of the Lord. I know you've all been thinking about it, so who wants to come up here first and share their ideas?"

A few hands go up. They walk up to the stage and line up.

The first kid says, "I thought we could do a food drive and help stock the soup kitchen. Then maybe they'll let us talk to people about God while we serve food."

The second kid is Kenny, the blond guy who invited me to his church.

"Right now my brother is fighting the war in Iraq. He said they really like getting letters. I thought we could start a pen-pal program to show them they aren't forgotten."

Suddenly I feel like crap for not having written to Pete in over a month. We talk on the phone every few weeks and I know my mom and dad email him. I've been so busy with the move that I've sort of ignored him. I'll write to him this week.

A tall upper-classman walks up to the mic and says, "I think we should put together a talent-show fund-raiser to raise money for sick kids who don't have insurance at the hospital. And after we've raised the money, we should go and perform for all the kids when we give them the check."

A few more students stand up and offer their ideas. "We'll choose a few of these ideas and announce them soon," Frank says. "Stop by and see me sometime this week to let me know which one you want to help out with."

As much as the being saved thing weirds me out, this whole volunteering thing is pretty damn awesome. If we do that talent show, I could do magic for the kids. Though I don't really like the idea of Christians trying to convert people while volunteering. I mean, what's wrong with Buddhism or Islam or not believing? I'm a good person. Most of the time. To me, all the gods out there sound like Santa Claus. It would be great if he were real but I haven't seen any evidence.

After the assembly I book it toward the door. I want to get home. I want to call Seth or Margaret and tell them about what I've just witnessed. I want to know what being saved means.

Chapter 5

I MAY NOT BE SAVED, BUT I'M NICE

That night I text Margaret and Seth and they agree. It's way different from our school in Mass. They think it's hilarious that I'm going to church on Sunday. And they're right. It's funny. Why would a kid who doesn't believe in god go to church? It sounds like the beginning of a bad joke. It's not. I need to make friends and if that's where the kids go, that's where I need to be. Otherwise, the next three years are going to suck.

Neither of them know what being "saved" means. I tell them about the girl's story and how god came to her or whatever. Margaret thinks they sound like they're in a cult.

I'm just about to Google the word *saved* when I look out my window and notice that Tess's light is still on. Her desk is in front of the window and I can see her sitting in front of her computer. I stand and start jumping and waving my arms to try to get her attention. After about two minutes when I'm almost out of breath, she finally looks up. She looks surprised for a second. Then mouths, "What?"

I point to the street and mouth, "Go downstairs."

She looks at me like I'm crazy and says, "No!"

"Pleeeeeeaaaaase," I say with my hands together.

Tess rolls her eyes, looks suspiciously to the left and right, and then holds her finger up as if to say, *one minute.*

I sneak downstairs and grab Holly's leash. If my parents figure out I'm gone, I can say Holly really had to pee. She looks a little confused, but excited that she gets an extra walk.

Tess takes a few minutes to come outside. We sneak away from the street lamp and sit on the edge of her yard, behind a big shrub.

"What could possibly be so important that you made me sneak out?"

"It's barely sneaking out. You haven't left your property."

"I'm cavorting with a known atheist. And a boy. It's a big deal to my parents."

"When you say it like that, it's like I'm a kitten killer or something."

"I don't think you kill kittens, and I don't think atheists are bad people. What you believe is what you believe. Be proud of it."

"Proud of my atheism? It is an *ism*, right?"

"Yeah," she says laughing. "It's an *ism*. It's a belief even if it means you don't believe."

"How would your parents know what I do or don't believe?"

"Obviously Angela told them."

"Does that mean they don't like me?"

"It's not that they don't like you. They just think you'll be a bad influence. I guess I could tell them I'm trying to save you."

"Okay, what does that mean? I had no idea what was going on at the assembly today."

"In that faith, it's not good enough just to believe in God. Jesus died for our sins and to truly be accepted into heaven and show our love we have to have our moment. Our moment when the Holy Spirit comes into our bodies and we have felt touched by the Lord."

"What if you don't get saved?"

"You go to hell."

"Jesus Christ. Are you kidding?"

"No. And when you're around me, please don't swear."

"Oh. At home it's not really thought of as a swear."

"It definitely is here."

"Sorry."

"That's okay. It's just good to know the ropes so you don't offend people. Especially the people who are nice to you." She smiles and pushes me in the shoulder.

Holly rolls over onto her back and Tess rubs her belly.

"What about Catholics and Jews and Hindus and everyone else?" I ask.

"What do you mean?"

"Where do they go when they die?"

"Hell. At least according to most people here."

"That's messed up."

"It's only messed up if you believe it," she says.

"You don't?"

She pauses for a minute, looks back at the house, and then straight into my eyes. "Look, I'm going to tell you something I've never told anyone but my brother. Can you keep a secret?"

"Yeah. Of course."

"I think the Christians around here have it wrong."

"But you still believe in god?"

"Yes."

"Do you think I'm going to hell?"

"No."

"Why not?"

"Because I believe that Jesus died for our sins and that counts for everyone. You don't have to be saved to go to heaven. We're all going no matter what we believe."

"You think your parents would be mad if they knew? You're still religious."

"They would think I'm going to hell and I don't want to put them through that. They've already lost one son. I don't want them to think they lost me too."

"They chose to lose their son. It's not like he died."

"It's really complicated. I know it's devastating for them but they don't want him to be a bad influence on the rest of us."

"Isn't it harder on your brother than it is on your parents?"

"Probably equal."

"Do you still talk to your brother?"

"I'm not supposed to but I email him all the time. I haven't seen him in two years though."

"Where is he?"

"Denver."

"That's not so far."

"It's really far when you're me."

"I'm sorry," I say, unable to think of anything else.

"Well, in a few years I'll be in college and then I'll be able to see him." Tess looks nervously back at her house. "I should get back inside," she says.

"Tess?" I say.

"Yeah," she whispers.

"Thanks for coming out here and for, you know, being so cool."

She smiles and moves her hair away from her face. "No problem."

Chapter 6

CHIMPS HAVE FEELINGS TOO

Tess and I hang out every lunch period for the rest of the week. She says that everyone knows I'm an atheist. No one has said a single thing to me about it and that's fine by me. Different beliefs cohabitating in the same school. That's how it should be.

No one besides Tess has really made an effort to get to know me. Kenny and the other guys I'm going to church with this weekend give me a high five or pat me on the back whenever we pass each other in the hall and say, "Sunday!" But that's about it. Back at home if someone did that, they would be excited about a Red Sox or Patriots game, not church.

We start getting homework assignments and things are pretty similar to my old school, although the teachers always seem to find a way to connect the day's subjects back to the Bible. It's annoying but I just ignore those parts. I even find that I'm not swearing. Without hearing it all the time in the halls, it's just fading out of my vocabulary. I'm even making an effort not to say Jesus Christ. Not because I think

I'm offending god or anything. I don't want to offend Tess.

The teachers seem pretty good. For our first book in English class, Mrs. Daniels gave out copies of *Beowulf*. I've already read the graphic novel version so it should be easy. We get to pick some of our own reading. Sadly, I doubt Mrs. Daniels would let me bring in *Bone* or *Y: The Last Man*. It's annoying that teachers still don't think graphic novels are real books. I've learned more about math from *Logicomix* than I learned from any teacher.

Up until Friday, I'm able to get by without offending anyone. I'm feeling like a model student. Even if I barely talk. Then Mr. Thompson, the science teacher, answers a kid's question about creation during fourth period.

Mr. Thompson says, "Scientists try to explain God's creation as something that came from a big pile of goo instead of from the Almighty. In my class, we're only going to study science that is proven and that hasn't been *poisoned* by evolution. You know," he says with a frown, "the belief that humans evolved from monkeys."

All the students in the room (except me) crack up like that was the funniest thing ever.

I raise my hand.

"Yes, Ben?"

"We did evolve. I mean, there is proof. I watched a documentary about it and they had all sorts of skeletons that show what human ancestors were like hundreds of thousands of years ago."

The class is silent. Mr. Thompson smiles at me.

"Ben, Earth is just under six thousand years old. That's when it was created. That's when man was created. That's fact. What you saw was scientific propaganda."

"But they have things like carbon dating that prove Earth is way older. Like a few billion years older. The creation stuff in the Bible is just a myth, right? I mean, every religion has one. A story that tells how the universe was created."

"And you believe you're related to primates?" he asks.

"Well, yeah."

The class starts laughing.

"You're new here, Ben, so you'll need some time to adjust. I recommend you pick up a book at the school library on creationism so you can get the facts down. Otherwise, you might find yourself saying incorrect things without meaning to. Because right now you're saying things that will get you a seat in detention . . . and in hell. And I don't think any of us want that, now do we?"

At this point, I decide to stop talking. I keep my head down and avoid eye contact with the rest of the class. I feel them staring at me. Like I'm stupid and maybe even a little bit evil. Like after class, I might just go sell some drugs in the cafeteria.

When class ends, I grab my stuff and get out of there as fast as possible. But not before hearing some kid making "Ooh oooh" monkey noises as I run by. Fan-freaking-tastic. I'm going to be the monkey-atheist kid heading for hell at top speed.

I'm going to have to do something to reverse my rep here. If I were Seth, I'd just be a starter on the soccer team and make friends that way. There is no magic club. I could start one, but I doubt anyone else would join.

So on Friday I go to Frank's office to sign up for one of the community service committees. I'll have something to do after school and be seen as a good guy at the same time. I knock on the door and he invites me in.

"Hi, I'm Ben. I wanted to volunteer for one of the committees for the community service project."

"Yeah, of course. Take a seat."

I sit down and he takes out a few lists attached to a clipboard.

"You're new here, right?"

"Yeah. Just moved here last week."

"Welcome. I think I've heard about you."

"Really? What have you heard?"

"How has everyone been treating you?" he asks, ignoring my question.

"Okay, I guess."

"Good. Good."

"Has anyone signed up for the pen pal one with people in the service?"

"A few," he says. "Is that the one you want to join?'

"No. Just wanted to see if people were doing it."

"Got family in the service?"

"My brother."

"God bless him," Frank says, smiling at me kind of creepily. I just nod awkwardly until he looks back at his papers and says, "What committee would you like to join?"

"I really liked the idea of doing a talent show for sick kids. Did that idea get chosen?"

"It did. Meetings start in two weeks. I'll be posting the schedule next week. These things take a lot of planning. I'm glad you're joining in."

"We didn't really have stuff like this at my last school."

"No fundraisers?" he asks.

"Well, we had a few bake sales, but the money always went to the school. I like that these projects help other people."

"That's what we like here. Service is a big part of this school. Whether it's worshipping the Lord or helping those in need, we're there. You know," he says, squinting at me intensely, "in case you were wondering, good deeds aren't what make you glorious in God's eyes. I mean, sure, He loves good deeds. But if it's heaven you're worried about, just accepting Him and worshipping Him is all He requires. Good deeds alone don't get you into heaven."

"Actually, I just really like volunteering. But thanks. That's, uh, really interesting."

"Well, if you have any questions about school or faith or anything at all, I'd like you to know that you can come talk to me."

"Sure. Thanks. Well, I should get to my next class."

"Thanks for stopping by."

I close his door behind me and shake my head. They really like reminding people about hell around here. How could it not matter whether or not you're a good person? What the hell does Jesus want from a kid anyway? If being nice doesn't even win me any points in this Christian town, how am I going spend the next three years here?

After school, Tess and I pick up her little brothers from the elementary school and walk home together. Angela stays late and plays basketball, so it's up to Tess to walk the boys home.

Every day, once we hit our street, I hang back while they walk to her house. Tess said, "It's just easier if they don't know how much we're hanging out."

Today her dad drives by as we're walking, stops the car, and says, "Kids, get in." Without hesitation, they do.

No, *Hello, new kid. Welcome to the block.* Not even a nod in my direction.

I walk the rest of the way home alone. About two minutes after I walk in the door my cell phone rings. It's Tess.

"I'm sorry about my dad."

"Yeah, well. It's a good thing he didn't hear me talk in science today. He might have run me down too."

"I told him you're going to church on Sunday."

"Was he impressed?"

"It was a start . . ."

"What do you mean by a start?"

"I kind of had to tell him that I'm trying to save you. And that you're into it."

"Okay, sure. If that gets him off your back."

"I wish it were that easy. He wants you to come to dinner on Sunday to prove your dedication."

"Crap. Seriously?"

"I wouldn't ask, but I won't be allowed to hang out with you anymore if you don't."

"Okay. I guess I'll be there."

"One more thing . . ."

"What?"

"It would be helpful if you started reading the Bible."

"You've got to be kidding me."

"You don't have to read much. Just enough to show that you want to learn."

I hesitate.

"We can do it together. I'll help you."

"Deal."

I hang up and immediately call Seth's house. He's going to laugh his ass off.

There's no answer. Then I call Margaret. Neither is home. I try Seth's cell. He picks up and I hear giggling in the background.

"Hey, dude," I say.

"Hey, man. What's up?"

"Nothing. Just calling to see how the first week went."

I hear a girl's voice in the background and then it sounds like the phone is being muffled under someone's hand.

"Hello?" I say.

"Yeah, Ben. Actually I've got to go. Busy night."

"Oh. Okay. Are you with Margaret?"

"Um, yeah. Look, I'll give you a call tomorrow."

I open my mouth to say, *cool, later,* but he already hung up. Uh, yeah. Missed you guys too. My week was strange and I have to lie to everyone in order to fit in. Thanks for asking.

Chapter 7

JESUS WAS A ZOMBIE

At 3 p.m. on Saturday, Tess comes over with her own Bible. Because we don't actually have one. I asked my mom and the best she could come up with was some self-help book about finding spirituality. Whatever that means.

My mom opens the door and invites Tess in. She asks Tess a few questions about herself. You know, the way annoying adults do sometimes. But Tess is like an adult expert. She's funny. She compliments one of the pictures on the wall and they talk about it. I mean, I'm polite with adults. Tess almost *is* an adult. She says to my mom, "Oh, really? A woodcut? The lines are beautiful." I don't even know what a woodcut is and the thing hangs in my house.

I give my mom a look that says, *enough*, and she takes the hint.

"Well, I'll leave you two alone. Let your dad know if you get hungry. He'll throw together some snacks. I've got a few errands to run."

As we walk upstairs, Tess asks, "Your dad cooks?"

"My dad is an awesome cook."

"Wow. My dad can hardly make a sandwich."

"He works from home, so it's easier for him to do stuff like that. Plus, my mom hates cooking. She'd order take out every night if she was left in charge."

"That's what my dad does when my mom leaves to visit my grandma in Lone Tree," says Tess.

I open the door to my room and Tess walks in ahead of me. She looks around, turning in a complete circle, and starts touching things on my shelves.

"What's this?" she asks.

"A poster I got at this show in Boston. They had the world's top magicians all together for one night. It was incredible."

"Wow. Can you do any of the stuff they do?"

"The really easy stuff. But their easy tricks for the average person are really hard, so it's still pretty good. My friend Margaret is better though."

"That's the girl you hung out with back home, right?"

"Yeah. She and I did magic together all the time."

"Were you guys, like, an item?" Tess asks.

"No. Just friends."

She sort of nods her head and then takes her shoes off and sits with her legs crossed on my bed.

I just sort of stand there. Do I sit next to her? Or on my desk chair? I mean, is it weird to sit next to a girl on a bed, even if it's your bed, and she sat there first?

"I could do some magic for you, if you want," I say, still standing.

"Um, Ben? How about you sit?"

She moves over and pats the bed next to her and then takes out her Bible.

This is the first time any girl other than Margaret has been in my room, let alone on my bed, and the first thing she does is take out a Bible. Fan-fricking-tastic.

I sit down a few inches away from her. She sighs and inches closer to me so that her knee is touching my leg. My heart is racing a bit and I'm not sure if she knows it. She doesn't look nervous at all. I'm so nervous that I'm starting to sweat.

"So, what do you know about the Bible?" she asks.

"Um, just what I learned in Catholic school. How Jesus was born and how he died, and then came back to life like some do-gooder zombie and then died again."

"Zombie?" she asks, shaking her head at me.

"A nice zombie."

She laughs. "That is so incredibly disrespectful. And anyway, he can't be a zombie because zombies stay dead. Jesus actually comes back to life. And he eats food. Not brains."

"I like that you're making an actual argument against Jesus being a zombie."

"It's kind of funny even if it's totally offensive. Just please please please don't say anything like that at dinner!"

"Okay. Well, what else? I know about Noah and how god killed people with a flood and with disease when he got kind of pissed off at humans."

"Wow. You really latched on to the important stuff, huh?"

"Some of those stories would make for a good horror movie. I mean, they talk about the people on the ark who were saved. Everyone else drowned and died a horrible gasping death. That's genocide. Shouldn't he have sent himself to hell for a move like that?"

"Well, that's the Old Testament. God was a little judgier in that one. What do you know about the New Testament? Do you know any of the Apostles? Or any of the Gospels?"

"Well, I only liked the bad-ass stories. The other stuff was kind of boring. I might have zoned out during those parts, if they taught them at all. It wasn't a super-religious school, not compared to here."

"Well, I'm going to give you a quick rundown of the highlights."

For the next thirty minutes, Tess starts talking about the New Testament like a teacher would. Totally full of facts and thoughts of her own mixed with stuff her parents and the church taught her. I feel like I'm cramming for a final exam. I even jot down a few notes.

After a while I get kind of bored, but Tess is so into it, so I decide that right now I've got a great excuse just to look at her. I don't think I was fair to her that first day we met. I mean, her hot sister was there so Tess probably doesn't get noticed as much around her. She's really pretty. She doesn't wear makeup or tight clothes like other girls so it's just not as obvious. She has hazel eyes, dark brown hair, and light freckled skin. And even though she wears baggy shirts, she still has boobs.

"Ben?"

"Huh?"

"I said, you're going to need a favorite Apostle. I was thinking you could like Peter since he's my dad's favorite. That okay for you?"

"Is it like baseball? You need a favorite team?"

"It will give you stuff to talk about, if he grills you on the Bible. And he might."

"It will be easy to remember anyway. That's my brother's name."

"Where does your brother live?"

"He's stationed in Iraq right now but he'll be coming here in December."

"That has to be hard for you."

"I'm here. It's easy for me. It's hard on him. I don't think his idea of being in the army turned out to be what he expected. He says there are two emotions in the desert. Bored and scared."

"I think I'd rather be bored," says Tess.

"Even when you're bored, you're still kind of scared, right? I mean, war is about waiting for bad stuff to happen, or knowing that it might happen."

"Your brother must be really brave."

"I don't think he has much of a choice. He makes a lot of jokes about it though. He says that for a bunch of eighteen to twenty-five-year-olds holding guns and facing the possibility of death, there is a surprising amount of laughing that goes on."

"People can't deal with being scared all the time," says Tess. "It would be too much. Making jokes must help keep their minds off the scary stuff."

"I feel bad sometimes. You know, I'll be doing magic or watching some stupid movie and I'll forget, for even like an entire day that he's over there. Then I feel like this bad person for living my life while he's risking his."

"It's exactly what your brother is doing though. Occupying his mind with something else because it's too hard to think of what could happen every second of every day. Don't feel bad about it. You need it. Otherwise you'd just sit here and worry." Tess kind of smiles sadly at me and puts her hand on mine and says,

"Soldiers want everyone to live their lives. That's why they're there, right? He probably just wants you to be a kid. "

We're silent for a few seconds and Tess's hand is so obviously on mine. I don't think either of us knows what to do, so she lifts it off and I say, "Can you leave your Bible here so I can read up on this Peter guy?"

"Yes. That's probably a good idea," she says, rubbing her hands together.

"You're my first friend that came with homework, you know that?"

"You're the first friend I've lied to my parents for."

"You win."

"So why don't you show me some magic?"

"Really?"

"Yeah. I'm interested."

"Prepare to be amazed. Or, you know, mildly entertained."

Chapter 8

SUNDAY IS CHURCH DAY, NOT SLEEP UNTIL NOON DAY

On Sunday morning, my mom wakes me up, sets down a respectable shirt and pants (because obviously I can't be trusted to dress myself), and tells me to get in the shower. I need to be ready in half an hour when Kenny picks me up for church. I just finish eating some cereal when there's a knock at the door. It's Kenny and his mom.

"Hi, Ben. I'm so glad you'll be coming with us today," she says. "I was hoping I could just say a quick hello to your mom."

"Sure, hang on." I run to the bottom of the stairs and yell, "Mom!"

She comes downstairs, whispers "Don't shout" as she passes by me and then puts on a big smile as she greets Kenny's mom. Kenny motions for me to follow him out to the car.

I feel a little overdressed. Kenny is wearing jeans and a T-shirt while I'm in khakis and a dress shirt. We get into the car and he introduces me to his dad, a tall, fat, bald man wearing a bowtie. There's some rock music playing, but the more I listen to the lyrics, the more I hear that even though it's rock, it's not the kind of rock I might listen to. It's rock devoted to god. All the same, I say, "Cool music."

"Thanks. This band is awesome. I'll burn you a CD if you want," he says.

His dad gives him a look.

"Actually, I can just lend you my copy."

Kenny's dad asks, "Have you ever been to a mega church before?"

"Just a Catholic church back home. It wasn't called mega or anything."

"So you're Catholic?" he asks.

"Um, well, not really."

"Perhaps you'll find that Southern Baptist suits you better, although there will be many different denominations there today."

Kenny's mom gets back in the car and we hit the road.

After about twenty minutes, I ask, "So, how far is this place?"

"It's in Colorado Springs, so about an hour away," says his mom.

"It's kinda far. Most people from Forest Ridge go. You'll see, it's awesome," says Kenny.

I kick off my shoes in the backseat and dig in for a longer trip than I expected. This place had better be impressive.

When we finally pull in, I see why they pass on the small church in town and drive out to this thing. The parking lot alone could be for a concert or a movie theater. It's huge. We ditch his parents and Kenny texts Stan and Arty to meet us in the front of the building. Now that I'm looking around, I see a lot of familiar faces. Tess wasn't kidding. Even though we're an hour away from home, everyone is here.

I walk in with the guys. We head over to the first seats we find open closest to the stage. Yes, I said stage. Not pulpit or platform. There is a microphone, drum set, keyboard, and guitar up there. This church could host a Coldplay concert. I can't even begin to guess how many seats are in here. Thousands?

Kenny, Stan, and Arty are talking about the school football team. They are all on it and from what I can tell, they think they're pretty damn good. They talk about plays and the coach and a whole bunch of other stuff before Arty realizes I'm just sitting there staring at the back of the head in front of me.

"You play any ball?" asks Arty.

"No. I'm not really into sports."

"What are you into?"

"I like magic. Games. Comics. Mostly, I like practicing new tricks."

"Cool," says Kenny. "Maybe you can show us some sometime."

"Yeah, sure. And I'll definitely make it to some games."

Kenny says, "So I've seen you around with Tess a bunch. Are you guys together?"

"Oh no. Just friends."

"She's cute though," says Stan.

"Not as cute as her sister," says Kenny.

"So true. Angela is smoking," says Stan.

"And if you tell her she's hot, she might meet you behind the bleachers."

"So, you guys can date?" I ask.

They laugh. "What do you think we are, dude?" asks Kenny.

"I just didn't know with, you know, your religion and stuff, if you were allowed to date."

"Yeah, man, we can date," says Stan.

There is an awkward silence for a minute. I'm trying to think of something to say but nothing comes to mind. Then I remember.

I say to Kenny, "That's awesome they chose your pen-pal idea. You know, writing to soldiers?"

"Yeah. My brother likes getting letters," he says. "Especially from girls."

"My brother is in Iraq too. He's coming home in early December though."

"Cool. Mine is coming home in mid-December. Just in time for Christmas."

"It's gonna be my brother's first time to Colorado. Maybe they could hang or something," I say.

A man steps up to the microphone and starts talking. The room immediately goes quiet. Everyone is focused on him.

The guy starts out decently enough, talking about scripture from some place in the Bible. Arty gives me a book and points me to the page. It's like opening *Moby Dick* in the middle. If you haven't read what comes before, you're not going to have a clue what's happening. Not that I've read *Moby Dick*, but my sister has.

Eventually he gets to the stuff I keep hearing about. How Jesus saves people. How we have a choice. The way he phrases it, it doesn't sound like we have much of a choice. It's more like, if you love Jesus, you're golden. If you don't, you might as well reserve your spot in the burning hellfire now.

He says either we can walk around like half-dead people with nothing good inside of us. That is to say, live without devoting our lives to Jesus. Or, we can accept Jesus and be happy.

I wish I could say I'm making this stuff up, but that's seriously what he's saying. That I'm half dead and not worth anything because I don't believe in god.

Now, I wish I wasn't here at all. In a room where everyone basically thinks I'm an awful person because I don't worship the god they worship. I don't worship anyone! (Maybe Houdini.)

The guy on stage goes even further and says that if you haven't been saved, you're an enemy of god. An enemy! Now that I'm in a room surrounded by people, thousands of people who think that I'll be bunking with Satan, it feels awful. Stan, Arty, and Kenny keep nodding their heads in agreement. At least when they aren't checking out the girls in the seats in front of us.

I look around and there are kids all over the place. Babies, toddlers, all the way up through teenagers. They come here every week and hear about how bad they are up until the moment they're saved. If I heard this stuff when I was five, I'd have been freaking terrified! Of course they say they believe in Jesus. The only other option is to be a half-dead enemy of Christ who goes to hell.

No wonder no one at school talks to me. I *am* an atheist. I don't believe this crap. I mean, a god? Really? And why this one? Why not any of the thousands of others throughout history? Cupid was a god once. Or worshipped as one. Now he just sells greeting cards. It's stupid.

After about forty-five minutes of talking and repeating the same things over and over—seriously, there is a ridiculous amount of repetition—the guy finally introduces the next act. A band goes up, the lights dim and here I am at 11 a.m. on a Sunday watching a rock concert. Everyone stands up and sings along to the music. It's like what was playing in Kenny's car. Rock music laced with the message of god. Kenny even does some fist pumping into the air.

I look for Tess in the crowd and eventually find her sitting with her family. Angela is a few rows over with a group of friends. Tess chooses to stay with her brothers. Her friend Beth is sitting next to her too.

Tess isn't swaying back and forth like other people, or giving the *I love you* look that other high school girls are giving the band. Parents stand, interested, but lacking the enthusiasm of the teenagers.

The band plays a few songs, there are a couple more prayers, and then, it's over. The band was way more fun than the sermon, but I couldn't imagine doing this every week. That preacher guy was basically saying I would burn in hell. Was he trying to scare me into believing? Or just shame me into it?

The preacher ends the sermon with a sentence that makes me cringe. He says, "If you want to know about having everlasting peace, come on up to one of our people and they'll direct you to someone who can talk to you about it."

Damn.

"We can wait around for a bit so you can talk to the preacher, " says Kenny.

"Maybe next time," I say carefully. "I don't want to hold anybody up. It's a long drive home."

"Your eternal soul doesn't like to wait. Come on. Don't be a coward."

Kenny grabs my arms and pulls me up toward the front, around the side of the stage and into the back. We stop in front of an office with the door open. He gives me a push into the room and then I'm standing in front of a preacher, a different one than the guy who spoke. He's smiling at me like a Miss America pageant contestant.

"Welcome. I don't think we've met. I'm Christopher."

"Uh. Hi. I'm Ben."

"Welcome, Ben. Would you like to have a seat?"

I look out of the office window to see Kenny smiling at me.

"Oh. Actually, my friend just wanted me to come in here, but I'm okay."

"If your friend thought you needed to see me, maybe you do. Have you been saved, Ben?"

"Oh god. I mean, um, well, I'm, uh, I've got to go. Thanks and everything. This just isn't my thing."

I awkwardly back out of the room. Christopher is still smiling his creepy artificial smile. I don't even look behind me as I shuffle backward and end up walking straight into Kenny.

"That was fast," he says.

"Yeah. I think it's a bit too soon for me. Maybe next time," I say.

"None of us knows when it's our turn. There won't always be a next time."

"Thanks, dude. I just, I think I want to get home. I've got a lot of homework."

Kenny shrugs and we walk back to the other guys.

I see Arty and Stan looking at Kenny, and Kenny giving them a disappointed head shake.

Kenny says, "So, church again next week?"

It all feels like being force-fed rotten Brussels sprouts and being expected to act like you're being offered cake.

"Let me talk to my parents. I'll let you know."

The guys are looking at me like they're let down. Like they really thought two hours in church was going to make me believe. Maybe if the preacher wasn't such a jerk to people who aren't saved, I could handle it. Spending two hours out of every weekend listening to some guy tell me I suck isn't fun. And if ten years of Catholic school didn't convert me, why would two hours of this? I mean, Catholics have hell and damnation too. They just get their point across with boring church music instead of with the Christian version of Nickelback.

Kenny, Arty, Stan, and I continue to shuffle through the aisle with all the other people to get outside. A few steps in front of us is that freshman kid who was sitting behind me and staring at me during the school assembly. He's holding his mom's hand. Just as I notice, I see that the guys are looking at him too.

Suddenly Kenny starts staggering and pretending that he's drunk. He even mimes holding a bottle up to his mouth to drink. The kid in front of us hears Arty and Stan laughing and turns to look back for just a second. Long enough to see what Kenny is doing, and then he speeds up a little.

"Dude," I say angrily.

"What? That kid's mom is a drunk. Plus, I think he's a queer."

"So?" I ask.

"Don't tell me you're a homo. Is that why you haven't hooked up with Tess?"

"I'm not gay," I say. In my mind I add *there is nothing wrong with being gay* but the words never leave my mouth.

Kenny says, "Man, you really do need to come to church. You're even worse off than I thought. A freaking fag sympathizer." Kenny stops walking, faces me, and takes hold of my shoulders. "I'm going to let you in on some truth, straight out of the Bible. Faggots are disgusting. They are filthy sinners and they should all be kept away from us normal people."

I remove his hands from my shoulders and say, "You've never even met a gay person, have you?"

"Heck no, I haven't. What do you think I am?!"

I want to tell him he's an ignorant, homophobic moron. Instead I flake out. I shake my head and walk back to the car without looking at any of the guys. I want to get away from them, but there are too many people, including the kid who they were teasing. I want to tap the kid on the shoulder and say *I'm not with them*, but he pulls his mom back into the rows of seats and heads for a different exit.

I keep walking and hear Arty say, "Maybe he's a fag too."

The car ride sucks. Kenny's parents ask me how I liked church and say they don't mind picking me up if I want to go again.

I say, "I can't next week but thanks." What I really want to say is, *did you raise your kid to be a bigot? Or did that massive, hateful church make him that way?* I still say nothing. My sister would think I'm a wuss. Maybe I am.

They pull up to my street. The first thing I do is look at Tess's house and think *damn*. I'm having dinner there tonight and I'm supposed to pretend to be on the road to conversion. It's either lie, or lose the only friend I've got.

I don't even know if Tess's version of Christianity is cool with gay people. What if she's not? What would I do?

Chapter 9

WWJD? PROBABLY NOT LIE.

At five o'clock, I walk across the street for dinner at Tess's house. I still have no idea what I'm going to say. I've thought about it. I even wrote down a list of things I could say. All of them either seem like lies or are way too truthful. I guess it depends on what they ask me. Maybe I'll grovel. Say something like, *religion isn't for me, but please please please please let me be friends with your daughter. She's the only person who's nice to me. Jesus was friends with a prostitute. Doesn't that mean she can be friends with an atheist?* Yeah . . . that's probably a surefire way to have them send me home before dessert.

I knock on the door. Tess answers. She sees that I'm not smiling, or maybe I just look like I'm going to throw up.

"What's wrong?" she whispers.

"I hated church."

"I think we both knew that was going to happen. You did it to fit in."

"They hate atheists."

"They just don't understand them."

I try to smile as Mrs. Colston walks toward us from the dining room.

"Hi there, Ben. So nice to finally meet you," she says. "Come on in and have a seat. We just finished setting the table."

I immediately go right to the best piece of *making parents love you* advice that Pete ever gave me and ask, "Can I help with anything?"

She looks at me approvingly and says, "No, I think we're all set, but thank you for asking."

Danny, Paul, and their dad are sitting at the table. I say hi to the boys. Danny asks me to do a magic trick but his dad hushes him.

I hold out my hand to Mr. Colston. He smiles and shakes it.

"Hi there, Ben. Tess has told us a lot about you."

"She's been really nice to me since I moved here."

"It's never easy transferring to a new school. My father was in the marines so we moved around quite a bit."

"Wow. My brother is in the army and he says the marines are tough. Did you make new friends?" I ask.

"I found the other kids with dads in the service and made friends with them."

I nod and there is silence for a moment. Tess is in the kitchen helping her mom.

"Is your brother in Iraq?" he asks.

"Yeah."

"How long has be been there?"

"This is his third tour. He's coming home for a break in December."

"God bless him."

"Were you in the service too?"

"No. My father wouldn't let me," he says. "I think the marines who saw World War Two from the Pacific didn't want their kids to go through what they went through. He said it was more important to get an education than learn to fight."

"My brother got both. He got his degree and then decided to give a few years to his country."

Tess and Mrs. Colston come in with plates of food.

"Tess, can you go get your sister?"

Tess runs upstairs and comes back down with Angela. She's wearing a skimpy top and, without even being able to control it, I look directly at her chest.

Mr. Colston says, "Angela, we have company. Go put on a sweater."

"It's hot."

"I don't care."

There is an uncomfortable silence as Angela runs upstairs, puts something else on over her tank top, and comes back down.

"Wonderful," says Mrs. Colston. "I think we're ready."

I make a slight move with my hand to serve myself, but Tess gives me a gentle kick under the table.

Everyone lowers their head and holds out their hands. Right. Praying.

I take Tess's hand and Danny's and bow my head. Mr. Colston starts to give thanks to the lord. All I can think about is how nice and soft Tess's hand feels. She's warm and she's not just laying her hand over mine. She's squeezing. I think my hand is beginning to sweat in hers and I know the thoughts now entering my head are probably not okay for the dinner table while grace is being said. I'm just glad I already put my napkin on my lap.

When Mr. Colston finishes his prayer, I let go of Tess's hand and feel my pulse start to go down.

The food is passed around the table and we all begin to eat. As I chew I start to freak out about when the questions are going to start. I eat each bite really fast so if they ask me something, my mouth isn't full of food. Instead, Angela is talking about her basketball team and how bad the freshmen are at free throws.

Eventually the conversation turns to me, and I'm ready for it. The church question. But it doesn't come. Instead, Mr. Colston asks me what my parents do and why we moved all the way from Massachusetts. They seem like pretty easygoing people. By the time we're done eating, I almost feel relaxed.

Tess clears our plates while Angela cleans some potatoes off her brother's chin. Mrs. Colston comes back in with three small dishes of ice cream.

She hands them to the kids and says, "Dan and Paul, I want you to go to the den to have your dessert. You can watch one television program and then you all need to finish your homework. Angela, you're excused."

"Are you sure? I can stay," she says, eyeing me.

"Go on upstairs. Now."

"Fine."

Mr. Colston just sits there, waiting for his wife to come back from the kitchen. I guess this is it. They didn't want to grill me in front of the kids. Or in front of fat-mouthed Angela.

Mrs. Colston puts a bowl of ice cream in front of each of us. Before she even sits down with her own dish, she says, "So Ben, I think you know why we asked you over here. We have some concerns. Would you like to speak on your behalf?"

"I'm not sure what you want me to say?"

"Well, we're curious about your feelings on Christianity and if you've decided to become a member of the church."

Tess looks at me and smiles. I smile back, feeling a little sick. When I'm quiet for about five long seconds, Tess says, "I told you, Mom. Ben was at church this morning. He wants to be saved."

"I'd like to hear it from Ben if you don't mind. Ben?"

"Yeah. Sorry. Tess is right. I did go to church this morning."

"And what did you think?"

My tongue is stuck in my throat. Lies or truth? Lies or truth? Lies or truth?

"Well, I um, I respect everyone's beliefs. And, you know, I'm glad I live in a country that gives everyone the right to think what they want. But I don't want to lie to you. That's not the kind of person I am and I hope you respect me more for saying this. Christianity isn't for me. I just, well, it's not how I was raised. But Tess is the best friend I've got here and I hope that my beliefs don't make you think I'm a bad person or anything."

Mr. and Mrs. Colston look at each other. Tess covers her face with her hands.

"What about church didn't you like?"

"It's not that I didn't like it. The music was good and the people were nice. I just don't believe in god or in heaven or hell. That's not to say I don't respect people who do. Tess is religious and I respect that. I would never question what she believes. The same way I would never want her to make fun of my beliefs."

"Son, you don't believe in anything. How are we supposed to trust a boy like that with our daughter?"

I stare at him for a few seconds with my mouth open. *I don't believe in anything?* What an ass. I was nice and he just totally says that like it's nothing? I want to yell back or say something obnoxious, but I don't. It's about Tess. Not about me. So I keep my cool. Or I try to.

I say kind of angrily, "I could have lied to you tonight. I could have said that Tess was trying to save me and that I wanted to be saved. I think it says more about me as a person that I told the truth."

"Well Ben, I hate to break it to you but someone here lied. Either you lied when you told my Tess that you wanted to be saved. Or Tess lied to us when she told us you wanted to be saved. So which is it? Are you lying to Tess or is my daughter lying to me?"

Oh crap. Oh no. He's looking at me and I have no idea what to say. He's right. I either just outed myself or Tess. Dammit! It should be me. I should say I lied.

I open my mouth to speak and then hear, "It was me."

I close my mouth and look over at Tess. I try to shake my head, get her to stop, but she just starts talking.

She says, "I found a friend. Someone I like and care about and he's here and knows nobody. The Christian thing to do is to be friends with him. I don't care that he's an atheist. That's his choice. And just because he believes something different than me doesn't mean we can't be friends. The truth is, he's nicer than most of the people we go to school with. And more honest about who he is."

Tess's dad looks furious. He puts his big hands on the table and glares at her. "So this boy who you think is so nice and considerate has you lying to your parents for him? Is that the Christian thing to do?"

"It was my idea to lie. I'm not turning my back on God. I'm making a friend."

"Tess," I say. "Stop. Just stop. Look, what if we promise to be honest with you from now on? I can't pretend to be someone I'm not but I can tell you the truth."

"How can I expect to be told the truth from someone who can't see the truth in front of his face."

"What truth?" I ask.

"That Jesus died for you. And you can't even say thank you."

"But sir . . ."

"But nothing. It's too important to disagree on. I'm sorry, Tess. I cannot let you spend time with this young man. The risk is too high."

"The risk of what?" I ask.

"I think we're done here. Ben, thank you for coming to dinner tonight and good luck at school."

"Dad, please. Don't do this."

"You know how I feel."

"It's like Michael all over again. How can you just cut people out when they think differently than you!?"

"Don't you dare bring him up. That name is dead in this house, and if you don't want to follow in his footsteps, you'll shut your mouth right now." He makes eye contact with me and says, "Ben, good night."

I look around the table. Mrs. Colston is staring at her plate. Tess's eyes are red and she's about ten seconds away from crying. Mr. Colston's face is firm.

I want to shout at him that he's an intolerant hypocrite who hates people who are different from him.

What kind of Christian does that make him? Tess is ten times the person he'll ever be. He's her father, so I say nothing. I stand up, put my hand on Tess's shoulder and say, "I'm sorry." As my hand leaves her shoulder, she starts to shake and by the time I'm at the door I hear her crying. I walk out and go across the street. Home.

I walk in the door to my house and head upstairs. I don't even stop to answer when my dad asks, "How did it go?" I slam the door as hard as I possibly can. Then I take one of the pillows on my bed and begin hammering into it with my fist. I punch until I can't punch anymore. I lie down on the floor and look up at the ceiling. Blank. No star stickers. This is not my house. This is not my room. This is not my life.

Chapter 10

GETTING OUT OF BED IS FOR SUCKERS

My parents don't bother me for the rest of the night. Which is a good idea on their part. I probably would have yelled at them for dragging me to this stupid freaking place. But they aren't so cool that they let me stay in bed the next day.

At 7:15 a.m. my mom knocks on my door, walks in with Holly, sees that I'm still in bed with my head under the covers and tells me to get my ass up. Well, she says it nicer than that.

"Sweetie, I know you had a rough night last night. But you've got to get up. School starts in thirty minutes."

"I'm not going."

"That's not up for debate."

"You're going to drag me out of bed?"

"If I have to."

"Go away."

I hear her sigh and then feel the bed dip down where she sits. Holly jumps up too and lies over the back of my legs.

"Want to tell me what happened?"

"No."

"If you want me to give you a mental health day, you're going to need to sell me on the fact that you need one."

"Tess's parents won't let us be friends."

"Why not?"

"Because I'm an atheist and I wouldn't lie about wanting to be saved. So now I have a total of zero friends."

"What about the boys you went to church with?"

"They're mean and hate gay people. And other kids at school aren't exactly lining up to talk to me."

"They just have to get to know you. Give them a chance."

"It's not about what kind of person I am. It's about what I believe."

"Okay. It's the beginning of the semester so I'm giving you one day to wallow. Tomorrow, you're going back. I don't want to hear a word about it."

"One day. Yeah. I'm sure my life will get better after one day. I hate it here."

"We all have to make adjustments. A new place is hard for everyone."

"You aren't being forced to go to a school where everyone hates you. I want to go home."

"This is home now. And I know it seems bad. It will get better."

I should thank her for letting me stay home. I should say that I hope she's right. Instead, I turn my head into my pillow and ignore her. Because at this moment, it's her fault I'm here. It's her fault that I left my friends back home. I just wish she'd go away.

She puts her hand on my back so softly it's almost as if it isn't there at all. Instead of making me feel better, I just hate her more.

"Just get out already. You can't fix this."

"Okay," she says, sounding hurt. And while a part of me feels guilty for making her feel bad, at least I'm not the only one. She gets up and closes the door behind her.

I go back to bed, this time with Holly curled up at my feet. My mom can stuff it, but Holly makes me feel better just by being in the room. She always does.

I wake up about once an hour, remember that there's no reason I should be awake and go back to sleep. At around noon I stumble downstairs and eat some cereal. On the fridge is a picture Pete sent us. He's in uniform giving some scraps to a skinny stray dog. I take the picture down and look at the back. It says, *My new friend One Eye comes by twice a day for breakfast and dinner.*

I go back up to my room and sit at my computer. I'm long overdue for an email to Pete. When I open up my mail, there is already an email from him. Bastard wrote to me first. Dammit! I'm such a crappy brother.

Kid,

It's 4 a.m. here. I have to be up in half an hour but I can't sleep. Mom tells me you're having a hard time in the new school. I wish I were there to set those loser kids straight. Instead, I'm here doing whatever it is we're doing. Keeping everyone safe, I guess. I can't tell you how much I miss Mass. I miss trees. You'd never even believe some of the places where I've found sand.

A bomber attacked a bus here yesterday. Twenty civilians dead. Five children. The longer I'm here, the less I understand people. I almost miss the simplicity of high school. You may get stuffed in a locker or sucker punched, but kids don't wind up dead. Not usually.

Anyway, just know that as hard as things are there, you're lucky. Lucky to be safe at home. I can't wait to get back there. To see you and Mom, Dad and Em. Hug Holly for me. There are so many strays here. They scrape by for food but lots of them look near dead. I saw one getting beaten and had to threaten the guy to let her go. She had stolen some bread from his stand. The Jean Valjean of freaking dogs. Poor goddamn thing. She looked starved. Same colors as Holly. I paid the guy for the bread and then bought her some dog food. Now she visits me every day. I sent Mom and Dad a picture. I wish they let us have dogs in the bunks. I'm thinking of opening a rescue shelter when I get back. For all the dogs like her back home. I'm sick of people, but I like these dogs more each day. Anyway, like I said, hug Holly for me.

And don't let the stupid stuff get you down. It's high school. Do your own thing and learn enough to get the hell out of there. I know it doesn't seem like it but that's what it's about.

Pete

No matter how big my problems seem, hearing from Pete always makes me feel like I'm a total self-centered turd bag. I don't want him to spend his time worrying about me so I write him something that downplays what I've been feeling. I write about Tess. But then I delete it. It's not like being in the army gives him a great dating life. And I don't want him to feel bad that he's in the desert without any of the things he used to like at home.

I keep it general and write:

Pete,

Mom is such a big mouth. You've got bigger things to worry about at 4 a.m. than me. You and I have one thing in common right now though. We both miss Mass. The crap I'm getting is different than what you probably dealt with. Everyone here is REALLY religious. And they think I'm a bad person because I'm not. But you're right. It's just high school. And even though I have to be here the next few years, I'm going to get through it whether people like me or not. I might as well go through swinging. So thanks, bro. Your emails always put my tiny world into perspective. I mean, you're in a goddamn war! That's serious. I'm just wussing out over not having friends.

Anyway, I scanned you a copy of the last *Ultimate Spider-Man*. Just remember, you may be an awesome hero, but you weren't bitten by a radioactive spider, so be careful.

Ben

PS: I hugged Holly and gave her a treat for you.

I send the email and then go hug Holly, who is still on my bed, and give her a treat. Then, I consider my options for the day. I could go outside and ride my bike. I could practice some new card manipulations. Or I could get ahead on my homework.

Normally, that last option would have been a joke, but Pete's right. If I want to get out of here, I have to make it happen. If I'm not going to have friends, the least I can do is make sure I get into a great college so I can be friends with anyone I want. I've always done my homework, but only enough to get decent grades. B's. Now, I want A's. I want to be smarter than every goddamn kid in that school.

I take out my homework assignments. First up is *Beowulf.* I pull the graphic novel off my shelf and start rereading it. I've got a paper due in two weeks. It's going to be the best damn paper I've ever written.

At dinner Mom asks, "So how are you feeling?"

"Better. But you don't have to email Pete every time I feel like crap."

"It's not every time. It was just this time."

"I don't want him worrying about me."

Dad says, "Your brother asked about you and your Mom told him a bit about what's been going on. He's far away. Knowing what's happening here, whether it's good or bad makes him feel like he's an active part of the family. He likes helping you."

"Well, he definitely helped."

"You're all ready to go to school tomorrow then? No more mental health days?" Mom asks, still looking a bit like I kicked her in the gut.

"I'm good to go."

After dinner I mess with some of the McBride moves from the DVDs that Margaret gave me. I think of texting them, but they haven't said a word to me and

I don't think I could handle any more disappointment from friends right now. At about ten o'clock I head upstairs to my room.

I sit at my desk and turn on my computer to check my email. When I look up, Tess is at her window waving her phone around. I look at my phone and see that it's still on silent from dinner last night and that I have like ten messages from her. I look up at her standing at the window and then text her.

"Hey."

"You weren't at school. I was kind of freaking out. You okay?"

"I just needed a day. You know?"

"I'm sorry about my parents. L"

"I'm sorry I got you in trouble."

There is a long pause. I glance up but I don't see her at the window.

"I missed you today."

Wow. She missed me. That must mean she likes me, right? Or does she miss me as a friend? Damn. Okay, my heart is beating fast and I need to respond.

"I missed you too . . ."

"Can you meet me outside later tonight?"

"But your parents . . . I don't want you to get in trouble."

"My parents are stupid and wrong. I only listen to them when they say stuff that makes sense, you know?"

"Eleven-thirty?"

"I'll be there."

At 11:25 I quietly put my shoes on. My parents sleep with the door closed, which makes sneaking out much easier. It's got to be way harder for Tess. She has to avoid waking up three siblings and two parents.

I open and close the door as softly as possible and head outside near that tree on her lawn. A few minutes later, Tess comes out. She waves for me to follow her. Without a word we walk along the side of her house and into her backyard. She takes my hand and leads me behind a small shed.

We stop walking and just stand holding hands. She looks embarrassed and lets go. We sit down on the ground facing each other.

"I'm sorry again about last night," I say.

"Why didn't you tell me you were going to tell the truth? It's just a bad idea."

"I didn't want to lie about who I am."

"You shouldn't have to."

"Neither should you," I say. "I just didn't think it all the way through. I didn't think he would figure out you lied just because I was telling the truth." She shrugs. "Can we talk at school at all?" I ask.

"Not with Angela around. And anyway, everyone goes to the same church. It would be hard to hide at school."

"But I want to see you."

"I'm right here."

"So we can only hang out in the middle of the night?"

"No. We'll just have to get creative. I can join the talent show. That will get us in the same room once a week."

"What happened last night after I left?"

Tess looks at the ground.

"Was it bad?" I ask.

"I'm grounded."

"Damn. I'm sorry," I say.

I put my hand on her knee and feel my pulse quicken. That's what people do when they care, right? Or will she just think I'm hitting on her? I guess I am hitting on her.

She puts her hand over my hand and says, "Isn't it awful that lying would have made our lives easier? That I can't even be honest with my parents?"

I know we're talking about something serious, but her hand on my hand has made it hard for me to listen. It's like my entire body is freaking out. I say as calmly as I can, "That's messed up."

"You don't ever lie to your parents?"

My brain (and other parts) is still buzzing but I focus. I now have no idea what to do with my hand. Do I leave it there? Do I turn it and hold hers? I'm such a freaking idiot. I have no idea what to do. Tess is looking at me and waiting for an answer to her question, and now I've forgotten what she said.

"What?"

She laughs and squeezes my hand. "I said, do you ever lie to your parents?"

"I guess sometimes about stupid stuff. Like, if I finished my homework. I'm definitely not supposed to be outside with you right now. Nothing like lying about my beliefs. They just want me to think for myself."

"If I tell the truth, they might hate me. Like my brother."

"They don't hate your brother," I say, feeling my pulse calm down.

"How do you know?"

"Your mom looked sad when you brought him up last night."

"Yeah, well, it was my dad's decision to cut him out. Not my mom's."

"Doesn't your mom have a say?"

"In their faith, the man is the head of the household. His is the final word."

"Seriously? That's effed. That's like, how things were a century ago, not now."

"Yeah, well, they believe women are supposed to be subservient to their husbands. And my mom is, even when it hurts her."

"Wow. Sucks to be a girl," I say. "And what about your brother? Did your dad cut him out right away?"

"He had already gone to college when he told them his feelings on religion, so he was out of the house and it wasn't as big a deal for him. I still have to live with my parents for three more years. I don't even know what they would do if I told them what I think."

"I think for now you've just got to keep going with the flow."

"You're not," Tess says.

"Yeah, but it's not my family I'm risking. It's just any kind of normal social life. And really, what kind of life was I going to have pretending to believe in god anyway? I'd be lying all the time. You at least believe in god. You're only partly lying."

"I guess. Lying to my family doesn't make me a great Christian though."

"You should talk to your brother about it," I say. "He'll get it. And we'll find ways to see each other. You're the only friend I've got out here."

She squeezes my hand and says, "Friend?"

"Well, um. Friend or something else?"

"I vote for something else."

I sit there, frozen. She's looking at me. Does that mean she wants me to . . .

"I really like you Ben."

"I really like you too," I say. My body is freaking out again.

"So . . ."

"Can I . . ."

"Yes," she says quickly.

"You don't know what I was going to say."

"You were going to ask if you could kiss me."

"And you said yes."

"I did."

Chapter 11

WHO NEEDS FRIENDS WHEN YOU HAVE A GIRLFRIEND

The next morning as I get ready for school, the fact that I have no friends doesn't bother me at all. I've got a girlfriend. A girl who is nice, smart, pretty, and thinks I'm awesome. I couldn't even sleep last night. Even though I didn't come back inside the house until 2 a. m. and had to wake up at seven. And now, I've had more than my first real kiss. I think we kissed for an hour. Which means I'm probably on kiss number three hundred and five. Hell. Freaking. Yeah.

I get to school and head to my locker. Not only do I have a girlfriend, but I'm also ahead on my schoolwork. Which pretty much makes me the most awesome kid in school today.

Or not. When I get to my locker, someone has written the word "FAG" in big letters. Underneath that, it says, "You're going to burn."

Wow. You've got to be kidding me. What the hell is wrong with these people?

I go to the bathroom, grab some paper towels and soap, and spend the next twenty minutes rubbing that crap off. It had to be one of the guys from Sunday. Kenny, maybe? I mean, who else would be so pissed at me?

Obviously, hating me is a popular state of mind because when I walk into homeroom, now late, no one even says hey. They all just keep talking in their little groups.

The teacher looks annoyed and says, "Do you have a note?"

"Sorry. I just had some trouble with my locker."

Kenny looks at me and smirks. I try and look away, ignore him. Any time I glance back, he's looking right at me with disdain. And why? Really, what have I done?

Thankfully, it only ruins my good mood for a little while. I just keep coming back to one fact. I've got a girlfriend. Seriously, I could just keep saying that same freaking sentence all day. So I ignore him. After a few minutes, I turn my chair so I'm not even tempted to look his way.

During my classes I barely hear anything the teachers are saying. I just go from room to room thinking about the night before. And when I walk in the hallways I just hope that I run into Tess. Not that we can talk or even really acknowledge each other's existence. But we'll both know. Too bad her locker is on the third floor and mine is on the second.

At lunch, I sit by myself. So far, not a single kid has even said hi. Arty walked by me and threw his bag over his shoulder so that it smacked me in the head. Then he laughed. I think being invisible would be better.

I grab my lunch and whip out *Beowulf* to read while

I'm eating. Every few minutes I look up to see if Tess is anywhere. Beth is sitting at their usual table. Tess isn't there. Angela is though. When we accidentally make eye contact she gives me a nasty smirk.

I feel someone walk behind me and then a little piece of paper falls onto my lap. I look around expecting to get smacked again or have something thrown at me. Instead the wormy freshman kid who Kenny called gay at church is walking fast out of the lunchroom.

I open the note and it says, *Meet me in the Ya-Zz stacks in the library*.

Maybe Tess sent the kid to come get me. Maybe she wants to make out in the library. Or maybe I'm about to get beat up in the stacks by some guys who made a poor freshman deliver the message.

I gather my stuff and go up two floors to the library. Of course it's empty. Now that I think about it, I should just come here during lunch. I can eat my food in the hallway on my way up and skip the cafeteria altogether. I won't feel like a loser and I'll avoid the pissy looks people feel like throwing my way.

I find the Ya-Zz section. It's in the back, far away from the info desk and totally private. I take out a piece of gum so Tess doesn't have to suffer through my peanut-butter breath. But Tess isn't there. It's just the wormy kid looking at me like he might vomit on my shoes.

"Hey," I say. I stand in front of him, waiting for him to speak. He just looks at the ground.

"You gave me the note, right?"

"Yeah."

"So, did you want to talk to me or were you getting me for someone else?"

"I, um, well, I just, um . . . ."

"Seriously, kid. You look like you're going to pass out. Calm down."

"The other kids say you're an atheist."

"I guess I am. Why?"

"You guess?"

"No, you're right. I don't guess. Yeah, I'm an atheist. Why? Are you going to try to save me?"

"No," he says looking me straight in the eye. "Because I am too." He breathes out like he's just confessed to murder. "I've never told anyone that before. I mean, I knew other people like me were out there. Until you got here, I'd never met one. So I've never been able to say those words out loud."

"You know if you hang out with me you'll look as good to the other students as a flaming bag of crap."

"You think they talk to me now anyway?"

"Your parents won't mind you hanging out with someone like me?"

"It's just my mom and she's drunk most of the time so she won't notice."

"Oh."

"Everyone knows. The church might be big, but you can smell her coming down the aisles. People laugh at her."

"They probably feel bad," I say, wanting to make the kid feel better.

"Not bad enough to help though."

"Have you talked to the preacher guy? Maybe he can help."

"She's been to rehab three times. It doesn't last. Anyway, I didn't bring you up here so you could feel bad for me. I just wanted to talk to someone who doesn't drink the Kool-Aid."

"I'm Ben," I say, holding out my hand, feeling oddly formal.

"James," he says, reaching out to shake back.

We sit down and James immediately starts throwing question after question at me. Kind of like Tess did. I guess they don't get many New Englanders over here. I tell him that where I live there are atheists, Jews, Christians, Muslims, all sorts of people.

"Not in this town," says James. "Just Christians and more Christians. You can't go an hour without someone mentioning Jesus. It's so annoying."

This kid has never met a Jewish person. Or a gay person. He's seen them on TV. That's it.

"It's like, you grow up and hear for so long that something is bad," he says, "that you think you're a bad person for thinking a different way, and then I meet someone like you and all of a sudden, those things I've been told are wrong are totally okay a few thousand miles away."

"Are you gay?"

"No. Those guys you were with think I am though." He leans in and whispers, "I like Beth. Tess's friend. But she's out of my league. Not that anyone here would date an atheist anyway."

"You'd be surprised who a girl would date," I say, smirking.

"In this town? Fat chance."

"So you've never met anyone else who didn't believe in god? Really?"

"Never."

"Well, welcome to the religious freedom club. You can believe whatever the hell you want."

"At church they say atheists are terrible people. That

they do terrible things and that they live their lives with a big hole in their souls where god is supposed to be."

"That's bull. Just because they don't understand what I believe doesn't mean I'm empty. As for doing bad stuff, don't Christians do bad things?"

"Yeah."

"Well, then they shouldn't talk. Most religions have the big stuff in common, right? Don't kill. Don't steal. Don't mouth off to your elders. Don't lie. Common sense stuff. It's just that I don't need a god to tell me that. I've figured it out on my own. I mean, you're an atheist and you seem like a nice kid."

He smiles, "I stole a comic book once."

"How did you feel after?"

"Not so good. I sent them money in an envelope."

"Because you were afraid of going to hell?"

"Because I felt bad."

"Exactly."

"Thanks, man."

"Sure thing."

"So you want to hang out some time?"

"Yeah. I do."

Chapter 12

STOP STARING AT GIRLS

or the next few days I barely see Tess at school. Every day when three o'clock hits we both go home and chat online while we do our homework. Sometimes we video chat and I get to see her in her horse pajamas. And then I make fun of her for wearing horse pajamas.

James and I hang out during lunch and he's actually pretty cool. Because his mom is out of it most of the time, he sneaks out and sees movies and buys comic books. I lend him a bunch of my graphic novels like *Maus* and *Bone* and *Y: The Last Man*. I think he stopped doing his homework and now just reads graphic novels. He comes by my house a few times a week for reading material and food. His refrigerator is usually on the empty side.

Even though I have a girlfriend who lives across the street, which might just be the coolest thing ever, I've only been able to see her once since the night we snuck out. Well, I see her at school, but we have to ignore each other. We met behind the shed one more time but we're trying to limit it to once a week. She's terrified of getting caught. Although g-chatting doesn't let us kiss, we do get to hang out for hours every night.

The odd thing is that Seth and Margaret haven't texted or called at all. Everything was fine when I left and I don't think I could have pissed them off from all the way over here. Whether or not they're mad at me, I'm mad at them now. We've been friends for years and they can't even tell me what's going on? That's just messed up.

At lunch, James tells me I should forget about them.

"They seem like crappy friends anyway."

"You don't understand. They were great friends. We'd hang out every day."

"Maybe they made new friends?"

"Seth has no idea how to make friends and Margaret is shy."

"You made new friends."

"I have two new friends. One I can't be seen with in public and the other is a kid no one else talks to."

"Thanks, man."

"You know what I mean."

"That I'm a loser?"

"That you have nothing in common with the kids in this school. Neither do I."

"So we're both losers."

"It's good. They leave us alone. You should actually do what Tess and I are doing."

"What?"

"Our homework."

"I do my homework. Most days."

"I don't just mean do it. I mean do it so well that they have no choice but to give you A's."

"Why? My mom barely remembers to look at my report cards."

"Because, those good grades will be your ticket out of here."

"You know my dad went here? He donated a bunch of money to the school before he died so my tuition is paid for. Which is good considering we don't have much money left. Definitely not enough for me to go to college anyway.

"You could just spend the next four years studying your ass off and get a free ticket to whatever school you want. I'm telling you, being smart is our way out of here."

After what seems like weeks, the first meeting for the talent show finally arrives. Tess and I can be in the same room without getting in trouble.

Frank shows up for the first few minutes to get us started. He puts a senior named Trent, the guy who originally suggested the idea, in charge of the group. There are about twelve kids in the room.

"Okay," says Trent. "First, I want to thank you all for being here. I can't wait to hear all of your ideas for the show. I talked to St. Mary's Children's Hospital yesterday and they said they would love to have us come perform for their kids. We scheduled our performance for December twelfth. That gives us two and a half months to prep. First, we're going to perform here for parents and friends as a fundraiser on December eleventh and then we'll take the show to the hospital and give them the money we raised. Now we're going to go around the room and I want to hear from each of you what you think you can contribute."

A group of three girls say that they want to sing and

dance. Four guys who have a Christian rock band want to play music. Another two kids want to do a dramatic version of a scene from the Bible. Seriously. While the drama kids give a detailed outline of their short play, Tess and I look at each other. Not obviously. But enough that she has to cover her mouth with her hand to stop herself from laughing.

I wish I were sitting next to her. We could be holding hands. That's what couples do. They hold hands and meet after class and have lunch together. They go to the movies. They try to sneak alone time in a house when no parents are home.

One day a month in this school you get to wear your street clothes and Tess is wearing a blue dress with a red cardigan. She looks awesome. Well, she's waving me off now instead of smiling. Why is she doing . . .

"Ben?"

"Yeah," I say.

"That's the third time I've said your name."

"Yeah. Sorry. Just was thinking about my project."

A few of the kids look at Tess and back at me and laugh.

"Great. Care to share?" asks Trent.

They all look at me intensely. Like they're really curious about what I'm going to say. Maybe they think my talent is going to be devil-worshipping.

"I want to put on a magic show," I say, pretending not to notice the kids laughing. "I can put on a ten to fifteen minute show."

"That's great, Ben."

The next sentence he kind of says to everyone but it's pretty obvious he's just talking to me.

"I don't think I need to tell you that all acts have to

be appropriate and family friendly. This show should make parents want to give money and make sick kids happy. That's why we're here. Now, Tess, you're last. What do you want to do?"

"I don't really have a talent I can do for the show. I thought I could be the stage manager. Make sure everyone has their props and give everyone their cue."

"That's a great idea, Tess. Thanks for volunteering for that. Also, the school choir has agreed to sing for the show. Now that we have the talent, we need publicity. We're going to meet every Wednesday after school for an hour from now until December to rehearse and promote. We'll make posters and think of other ways to get the word out. Sound good?" Everyone nods. "You're all dismissed. Have a great day and start working on your talent."

The students all put their stuff away as fast as possible. Only Tess and I take our time. Trent packs up his backpack and when he gets to the door he looks back at me and Tess, smirks, nods, and then closes the door behind him.

Tess turns red.

"Are we that obvious?" she asks.

"I didn't think so, but more important Trent is a good dude. "

"Yeah. He's always been really nice. He actually went out with Angela. He dumped her after he found out that she's, you know, mean."

I put my bag down, walk over to Tess, and kiss her. She wraps her arms around me for a minute, then pulls away.

"We shouldn't be in here," she says.

"The teachers are gone. The other kids are gone." I lean in to kiss her again.

"I just . . . I don't want to risk it," she says, pulling farther away. "And I need to go get my brothers."

"You're such a good older sister. I'm lucky. I've just got older siblings so they had to take care of me."

"You only ever really talk about your brother. What's your sister like?"

"She's cool."

"Where is she?"

"At college."

"You never talk about her," says Tess, pouting.

"Not much to say. I mean, she's great."

Tess gives me an exasperated look. "Okay, I've got to go."

"All right," I say, letting go of her hand.

"You're not going to try to talk me into staying longer?"

"You've got to get home. I understand," I say, happy to stop talking about Emily.

"You'll see me in an hour on g-chat," she says with a grin.

Tess looks at the classroom door and then leans in for a quick kiss.

She smiles. "See you later."

Chapter 13

GOD AND SCIENCE GO TOGETHER LIKE PEANUT BUTTER AND TOENAILS

For the rest of September, Tess, James, and I get straight A's. Tess isn't great at math but James is a numbers freak so he helps her out, even though he's a year below us. I'm pretty good at science, which isn't James's best subject, so I talk him through some of the geology stuff he's doing in Earth Science. Because I have James to hang out with during school and on the weekends, I don't even really care that the rest of the kids completely ignore me, and sometimes make chimp sounds when I walk by. At least nothing else has been written on my locker.

Once or twice a week during lunch, Tess sneaks up to the back section of the library to hang out with us.

Luckily, Tess seems to have forgotten that I've got a sister. She hasn't asked me anything about Emily. Which is good. What do I say? *My sister has a girl-friend. Hope your god doesn't mind.*

It isn't until the second week of October that I hit my first real snag in the whole getting-perfect-grades plan.

The first few chapters of the science textbook are all about plants and Mr. Thompson sticks to asking questions about the facts. I mean, he calls everything *god's glorious creation*, but then he goes on to talk about true stuff like photosynthesis. When we get to the next chapter on human biology, it gets to be less about facts and more about the Bible. What the Bible is doing in a science textbook, I'm not sure. But there it is.

Mr. Thompson asks, "Now that we've talked about the circulatory system, and how it is critical to respiratory function, I want us to look at the bigger picture. Who here can tell me what the Bible says about blood?"

A bunch of hands go up in the air.

"Ben, your tests and labs have been excellent, but we haven't heard much from you this semester. Tell me what the Bible says about blood."

"Can I answer a question about blood instead?"

"No. We've gone over red blood cells, white blood cells, platelets, veins, and the heart. Now I want to talk about what it all means."

"I'm not sure."

"Didn't you read the chapter?"

"I did."

"It says it in the first paragraph."

"I'm sorry sir. I don't remember."

"Well, try to think of your own Bible reading. Maybe you'll remember that way."

I try thinking back to my days at Catholic school. The cracker is the body and the wine is the blood. What does that mean about blood and the Bible? Damn it.

Kenny raises his hand and says, "I know."

"Thank you, Kenny, but I'm not asking you. Mr. Pinter, can you tell us anything? I know you read the material, but perhaps you're missing the larger point of all of this. Science is about celebrating God's Creation. It's another form of devoting ourselves to Him and reveling in His workmanship."

"I'm sorry, Mr. Thompson. I really don't know."

"And why do you think that is?"

"What?"

"Why do you think you ignore the religious teachings in the textbook?"

"The facts are all I need to know. Facts are the basis of science."

"The Creator is the basis of science. You need to start paying Him some attention or you're only going to understand the bare minimum required for this class. Anyone else?" he asks. "Can anyone tell me what you learned in your reading about blood?

Without even raising their hands three kids, including Kenny, call out "the life of the flesh is in the blood."

"And what does that mean?" he asks the class.

"That Jesus died for us and with his sacrifice comes our purification."

"Excellent," says Mr. Thompson.

When lunch hits I feel sick to my stomach. I mean, how can knowing the facts not be enough? That's what science is. Facts. Science is about discovery. If I wanted to study air travel, I wouldn't start my research by looking at pictures of Santa's flying sleigh.

Luckily, Tess is sitting with James in the library when I get up there.

She sees me and asks, "What's wrong?"

"Mr. Thompson sucks. He called on me in class today and asked why blood is important in the Bible. I had no idea."

"It's the life of the flesh," say Tess and James almost at once.

"What does that mean?!"

"In Leviticus it says, 'the life of the flesh is in the blood,'" says Tess.

"Wait. Isn't Leviticus the one that says gay people are bad?" I ask.

"Yeah," says James.

"No wonder I haven't paid closer attention to that freaking masterpiece."

"Hey," says Tess. "I know you're mad, but try not to Bible bash."

"Only if the Bible stops gay bashing."

"Look, the Bible is an old text. Thousands of years old. It doesn't just say gay people are bad. It says slavery is okay and a bunch of other ridiculous things. I know it's outdated. The founding fathers of this country owned slaves too. It's not okay today, but it was considered okay back then."

"Will that argument work with anyone around here who isn't you?"

She relents, "Most people around here think the Bible is true word for word."

"Then I'm allowed to be pissed, right?"

"Yes. Just try to be *peeved* without trashing my religion."

"I'm sorry. It's just hard."

"Why? I mean, it's not like you know any gay people."

I give her a look, like, *really? Are you sure?*

"I mean, I don't know any," she says.

"I'm from Massachusetts, remember? Not from the town of Homophobe in Bible Belt USA."

"We're not all that way. I'm not."

"How was I supposed to know that?" I ask angrily.

Tess looks hurt for a moment. Then turns on me and says, "So you assumed that I was hateful?"

She stares me down, her arms folded.

"My sister is gay," I say.

"So you thought I would think your sister was a bad person because she's gay?"

"I guess I wasn't sure if you'd be cool with it or not."

"You weren't sure?" she says, looking furious.

"You can't really blame me! I mean, everyone around here thinks gay people are evil sinners, don't they?"

Tess grabs her stuff, gives me a nasty look, and storms off.

"Dude," says James.

"Shut up."

"Will do."

Chapter 14

SURGICALLY REMOVING FEET FROM MOUTH

When I get home from school, Tess isn't online. The curtains are down in her room so even though her lights are on I can't wave to get her attention. It's Thursday and usually on Thursdays we meet outside in the shed, but something tells me that tonight I shouldn't bother sneaking out.

Instead I call Emily.

"Hey, Bro! How's it going?"

"Bad," I moan.

"Why bad?" she asks.

"Well, I have a girlfriend."

"Seriously? Since when?"

"About a month."

"And you didn't tell me? Is it that Tess girl you're not allowed to see?"

"How do you know that?"

"Dad's a talker."

"Yeah. Well, we've been sneaking around and

talking online. But we don't get to talk about stuff in person very often and there are certain things you just don't want to say online, you know?"

"Like what?"

"So she's Christian, but not crazy Christian like everyone else. I didn't know how she felt about gay people. Then I made a comment about the Bible being homophobic and she thought I was calling her homophobic."

"Did you tell her you have a gay sister?"

"I didn't tell her until today cause I didn't want to tell anyone until you had told Mom and Dad."

"While I appreciate your loyalty to me, here's some advice. If you don't know how she feels about something, ask her. If you think she's trustworthy, then trust her. Otherwise you're thinking for her and no one likes that."

"So I should say I'm sorry?"

"Yes."

"That's what I thought. So how is married life?" I ask.

"We're good. School is great. I love it here."

"You'll make it fun when I come visit, right?"

"Of course. Although it's probably when I'll tell Mom and Dad. So I'm not sure how much fun they're going to have."

"They'll be fine. Didn't you just give me that whole speech about trusting people? Shouldn't you trust them? I think they've earned it."

"It's just hard. I mean, I don't want them to think about me getting it on with anyone, male or female, but when I tell them, that's exactly what they're going to think about. I don't want them imagining me making out with my girl . . ."

"Stop talking! I don't want to imagine it either, so just stop talking."

"See! Totally embarrassing."

"Suck it up."

"I've got to go. Lots of reading to do for class tomorrow," she says.

"Have fun with that."

"Who doesn't love Anne Carson? Of course I'll have fun."

"Whoever that is. Later, Em."

Tess might not be signed into chat, but I bet she's up in her room. I send her a text. *I'm sorry about today. Can we meet tonight so I can explain? Please?*

Hopefully she'll agree to see me.

I look over at Margaret's DVDs next to the bed. I haven't been practicing much but I need to start. Otherwise, I'm going to look like a fool at the talent show. I'm really good at up-close magic, but in front of an audience? That's a whole different set of illusions.

I grab my fanning powder and give my cards a light fresh coat. Then I turn on the DVD to learn how the hell to do the kind of card manipulation that's going to make people's mouths fall open.

I can do a few of the easier moves without too much trouble. Margaret taught me those in seventh grade. So I start with the harder stuff like Cardini's cards, packet vanish and interlock production. I've seen Margaret do those but I haven't worked on them so my hands are clumsy. Practice is the only way to sink this show. So that's what I do.

About an hour later I get a text. It's Tess. *I'll see you at the shed at 11:30.*

A little cold but she'll be there. I spend the next few hours watching McBride do things with cards I can only dream of. As I watch I write down a basic outline for which illusions I'm going to use for my performance. Then I start pounding away at them. It's like doing layup drills during basketball practice. You've got to keep doing the same move if you're going to get good at it. And I need to be great.

At dinner I'm kind of quiet. When my parents ask me what's wrong, I say nothing and keep eating my pasta. My mom sort of rolls her eyes and looks at my dad. They probably just think I'm being a sulky teenager. The way Emily got when she was my age. So they let me eat without bothering me anymore. Instead, Mom talks about Pete and how excited she is to have him home in December. Not for good, but for a while.

He'll get to wear regular clothes and see movies and eat food he actually likes. Mostly, when he's been back twice before, he's pretty quiet. He doesn't go out and hang with his old friends very much. He stays home, reads books, and watches movies. He says, "When you're in the army, you're lucky if you get to take a shit in private, let alone be in a room by yourself all night." I don't think I'd have it in me.

After dinner I go back upstairs and practice some more. I mess with the different illusions until my fingers start to cramp. These tricks are rough. It's going to take a lot of work to master them. It would go faster if I had someone to work with. Someone who was already good at them and could show me the technique and fix my hands when I'm doing something wrong. I need Margaret. I think about calling her but it's time to meet Tess.

I sneak downstairs and open the door. "Going somewhere?" asks my dad.

"Jesus. You scared me."

He stands up from the chair in the living room and turns on a light.

"This is the third Thursday night I've heard you go outside."

"And you didn't stop me?"

"I watched from the window. You went across the street. I get it. You're fifteen and you're not allowed to see your girlfriend."

"How do you know she's my girlfriend?"

"Because I'm not an idiot."

"Does Mom know?"

"Not about the sneaking out. You know your mom. She sleeps like someone hit her over the head."

"We're not doing anything bad. It's just the only time we can see each other."

"If Tess gets caught, you know she's going to be in a lot of trouble, don't you?"

"Yeah."

"So maybe this should be the last time you meet in the middle of the night,"

"How will we see each other?"

"I know it's not fair and I know you've been dealing with a lot since you got here, but sneaking out isn't the way to solve it."

"How do I solve it?"

He shakes his head. "I don't know. Religious differences are a tough nut to crack. But it will get better."

"That's all you've got for me?"

"Yep. You go tell Tess you can't meet like this anymore."

"It may take a little while. I also have to apologize for something else."

"Stuck your foot in your mouth?"

"Up to my knee."

"Okay."

"Night, Dad. And thanks."

"I was fifteen once too."

My dad heads back upstairs and I hurry across the street to the shed.

"You're late," says Tess.

"My dad caught me."

"Oh no!" she says, forgetting for a second that she's mad at me.

"He was cool about it, but this is the last time I can meet you out here."

She slumps her shoulders and looks at the ground. "When will I see you?"

"We'll figure it out."

We both sit down on the ground. Now that it's October, it's a bit colder. She puts her head on my shoulder and I wrap my arm around her.

"About earlier," I say. "I'm sorry. My sister told me that she's gay, like a month ago. My parents don't even know yet."

"That's big."

"I mean, it shouldn't be big. It's just who she is, but it's new. Not new to her. New to me. And then at church the guys were gay bashing. Kenny wrote fag on my locker and it made me want to punch him in the face. All of a sudden there were these people who don't like my sister, and they've never even met her. I feel bad that she never said anything in high school because she was worried about what people would think. When you meet my sister, you'll know that it's rare for her to care at all what other people think."

"It's never easy being different."

Tess hugs me tighter.

"I just worried that growing up around here, you might think horrible things about gay people and I didn't want to risk telling you and having it go badly."

"You're just going to have to trust me, okay?"

"I'm sorry I didn't."

"You should go inside. Your dad will probably be waiting to hear the door."

"I think he can wait a few more minutes," I say, smiling.

"Just a few," she says and kisses me.

Chapter 15

AT LEAST ROMEO AND JULIET HAD A FRIAR ON THEIR SIDE

I head up to the library to meet James. Unfortunately, the first quarter is almost over and any student who cares about grades has been in the library during lunch. Tess can't show her face around us or someone will tell Angela who will then tell her parents. We haven't been able to sneak out since my dad caught me, so we talk online, see each other at the talent show rehearsals, and that's about it. Even at the rehearsals we can't work together or speak unless it's about props or publicity. It's torture.

Angela shows up at the meetings a few times to ask Tess something. Then she stays and tries to talk to Trent. And frankly, Trent looks less than interested in spending time with her. It makes me wonder . . . could Trent be an ally?

During the next rehearsal I ask Trent if he can hang around to talk for a few minutes when we're done.

"Yeah, sure," he says, looking at me curiously.

After everyone, including Tess, clears out, Trent sits next to me.

"What's up?" he asks.

"This is kind of awkward."

"You're not bailing, are you? We only have six acts and we need them all."

"I'm not bailing."

"Okay then. What?"

"I think you've probably figured out that I like Tess."

"And that she's into you too. Angela told me."

"Right."

"But you guys aren't supposed to see each other," he says.

"Right."

"Look, I personally don't care that you're an atheist. But Angela has it out for you. She's asked me a few times if you guys have been talking in here."

"We haven't."

"I know you haven't. You do stare at each other whenever you don't think people are looking."

"Have you told Angela?"

"No. And I'm not going to."

"Does that mean you might be willing to help us?" I ask.

"Help?"

"That first day, you left Tess and me in here alone and closed the door behind you. That was really cool."

"Look, I don't know you. I know Tess and she's a really nice girl. Her sister is kind of a monster but Tess is great. If she wants to be with you that's her business. I'm not looking to get in the way."

"But you won't help either."

"What kind of help?"

"I don't know. Just assigning us to work together."

"Kid, no offense, I've got bigger things to worry about than you and your girlfriend. I won't get in your way but I can't be your ticket to see each other."

"Okay. Thanks anyway."

I pick up my stuff and head toward the door.

"Hang on," he says.

"Yeah?"

"The backstage space in the auditorium is completely empty when it's not being used for rehearsals. No one ever goes back there."

I smile and nod at him. "Thanks, man."

"Just be cool to her, okay?"

"Definitely."

He grabs his bag and turns to leave then stops, looks back and says, "I'm looking forward to seeing your act. You sound like you know what you're doing."

Trent walks out the door. Instead of heading home, I go straight to the auditorium. Better to explore it when no one is around than risk getting caught tomorrow. If Tess and I really can use the space to see each other, we'll get to have a semi-normal relationship. Even if meeting on school grounds is risky.

The auditorium is empty. I jump up on the stage and look out at all the seats. This is going to be where I perform my first magic show. Freaking awesome.

I open my bag and take out my cards. It's a good idea to carry a deck around with you. People love impromptu magic shows. Or they did at my old school. Some kid would ask me to do a trick in the hall and then I would riff off into another trick. I'd keep it going until I had ten kids around me, and the bell would ring.

The thing about magic is that it's fifty percent skill

and fifty percent personality. You have to smile, entertain, and make the audience feel like magic could possibly be real.

Not here though. No one but James and Tess wants to see me do anything. Well, the suckers will have to pay attention to me during the show. Moms and Dads and kids from the school may not like me, but they're going to like the show. I just need to make sure that I'm perfect.

I head backstage. Trent was right. It's huge back here. There is a dressing area, a massive closet full of costumes, a make-up table, the green room, and two huge bathrooms. Well, the guys' bathroom is pretty standard. The girls' bathroom has a bunch of couches and chairs.

I know. I probably shouldn't be in the girls' bathroom.

The best place for Tess and me to hang out would probably be the costume room. There are tons of racks of clothes to hide behind just in case someone came in.A part of me wants to tell Tess. The other part wants to stay in the auditorium and go through my magic show in my mind. Get a feel for the stage. So I do. Even without my fanning powder, I go through the show, try and move around like a rock star would on stage, and mentally prepare to perform in front of hundreds of people who really don't like me very much.

I try a few times but I keep blowing the illusions on the harder moves. So I do the only thing I can do. I call Margaret. She'll be able to help me. If she answers the phone. I call her home phone instead of her cell so she doesn't know it's me.

"Hello?"

"Hey Margaret."

There is silence.

"Margaret?"

"Hey, Ben. How are you?"

"That's what you have to say? It's been a month and a half!"

"I know. I'm sorry."

"What happened?"

"Seth and I are together now."

"Okay. That's great for you guys."

"He's jealous."

"Of what?"

"We kissed, remember? He was right there."

"It was a dare. It was part of a game."

"Yeah, but . . ."

"But?"

"Then I gave you my McBride DVDs."

"That was awesome of you."

"Seth didn't think it was awesome."

"Why?"

"He knew that I liked you."

"Oh. I didn't know that."

"I know you didn't. But Seth did. And once you left he asked me out and we've been together."

"He doesn't want you talking to me even though we've been friends since sixth grade?"

"Yeah."

"Well, that's a load of bull."

"Ben, you can't—"

"You guys just dropped off the face of the earth! I moved away, my life turned to crap, and you guys won't talk to me because Seth is jealous? Friendship should matter more than that kind of stuff."

"I'm sorry."

I take a few breaths and calm down.

"I'm really happy for the two of you," I say.

"Thanks."

"Think Seth would feel better if he knew I had a girl-friend?"

"You do?"

"Sorry. Was that insensitive?"

"No, you jerk. Thanks for the consideration. I'm totally over you."

"Um, who's insensitive?"

"What's her name?"

"Tess."

"And how is the new school?"

"Pretty much every student besides for two ignores or messes with me. Tess's parents won't allow her to date an atheist so we're keeping our relationship secret and can't really see each other even though she lives across the street. The good news is, I met another atheist and he's allowed to hang out with me, mostly because his mom is too drunk to know that her son has left the house."

"That's quite a new life you lead. Since when do you call yourself an atheist?"

"Since I realized that not believing in god makes me one and that religious people, well a lot of them, don't like me for it. But that's not why I'm calling. I'm doing a magic act for a fundraiser talent show and I can't get some of the card manipulations right. I need your help."

"You know that talking to you right now is going to make Seth jealous."

"Seriously, are you going to let a guy tell you who

you can talk to? Especially one who is being a total ass."

"Don't call Seth an ass. He's insecure. You know that. And he's your friend."

"He's not my friend if he won't even talk to me. He's being a tool and you know it."

"Okay, I'll help."

"What are you doing over Thanksgiving?"

"Eating."

"Can you teach them to me then? I'll be back home and we can practice in person."

"Only if you can fix things with Seth before then," she says.

"Deal. Then maybe you guys can be my friends again. As long as you've gotten over thinking about how sexy I am."

"Shut up."

"I'll try."

"Talk soon," she says.

I hang up and start putting stuff back in my bag, but I see something that doesn't belong to me. It's James's science textbook. That means that he has mine.

Damn. I guess I'm not going home right away.

After I finish packing up my stuff, I walk over to James's house. I've never actually been here. My mom and I dropped him off late one night but you couldn't really see the place. All the lights were off.

It's not exactly the nicest looking house I've ever seen. The paint is chipped and there are a bunch of overgrown weeds out front. I knock on the door and wait for a few minutes. No one answers. I knock again, a bit louder, and this time I hear something. There's a loud crash and then the door opens.

A woman in a raggedy, partly see-through nightgown answers the door. She's not wearing a bra and I kind of stumble back a step or two and do my best to look at her face.

"What do you want?" she says, looking at me through squinted eyes. Her breath reeks of alcohol.

"Oh, I'm uh, looking for James."

"He's not here."

"Do you know when he'll be back? I have his textbook."

I hold it up and she looks at it closely, like I could be lying or something.

"Leave it on the step," she says. "He'll see it when he gets home."

"Oh. Okay. I'm Ben," I say, not really knowing what else to do.

She turns around and closes the door.

Damn. James said she drank. I had no idea it was going to look like that. I stand there for a few minutes, dumbfounded. That is, until I hear a voice say, "Dude? What are you doing here?"

I turn around and see James walking up.

"I have your book," I say. "I think you have mine."

He looks at me kind of suspiciously.

"Did you knock?" he asks.

"Yeah."

"Did she bother to get up for the door?"

"Yeah."

He kind of shakes his head and sits down on the step.

"I didn't know it was that bad," I say.

"She's not mean or anything."

"That's good," I say, not really knowing what else to say.

"Was she dressed?" he asks.

"Partly."

"Great."

"You know you can always crash at my place if you want to. My parents like you, maybe more than they like me."

"I don't think she'd even remember to eat if I wasn't around. The only things she does consistently are drink and go to church. Funny, right?"

"I'm sorry."

"Can't have everything. Before this year I didn't even have any friends. So I figure stuff is getting better."

He takes out something from his backpack and holds up a test marked 95.

"We're getting out of here, right?"

"You know it."

"You have any food in the house?" I ask.

"Cereal. Stuff like that."

"Let's walk down to the diner and get some dinner," I say. "We can pick something up for your mom too."

"Thanks man."

"Anytime."

Chapter 16

COSTUME ROOMS AND WEDDINGS

The next day at school I wait for Tess in the costume room at lunch. She was so excited when I told her I had a place we could meet. James has to sit in the library by himself, but he's got a lot of work to do. Plus, he knows how sucky it's been for Tess and me. Not that he doesn't have his own problems. Or that he doesn't get all whiny about how Beth never even looks his way.

Just like yesterday after school it's empty back here.

I hear the door open and I half hide until I see that it's her. She looks nervous. Then she sees me and smiles the biggest smile I've ever seen.

I don't say a word. I just walk up to her and kiss her.

It's so much better than hiding behind her house. We put some of the clothes on the floor so we can be more comfortable. I almost suggest we move to the girls' bathroom to hang out on the couches, but I'm too afraid someone will need to use it. Here it's like the jungle. We have cover. Even where we're sitting is a hiding spot. For the next ten minutes all we do is kiss. It's glorious.

Then she breaks away and gives me a sad smile.

"What's wrong?" I ask.

"Just family stuff. And friend stuff."

"The sneaking around?"

"That's part of it. Beth keeps asking me about you. She knows we hung out the first week of school and that I liked you, and now she thinks I'm acting weird."

"She's your best friend. Maybe she'd be cool with it."

"She's pretty into the church. I mean, I don't know what she'd think of me dating an atheist."

"James kind of likes her."

"Really?!" Tess asks.

"Yeah. She's not cool with atheists?"

"I don't know. I mean, she's not as hardcore as some other people. She's very devoted to God."

"Are you worried she won't be okay with you being with me?"

"I just don't want to lose a friend."

"I think you should give her a chance."

"There's another thing. My brother. He told me something yesterday and I feel both really happy for him and really awful."

"What did he say?"

"He's getting married. I'm going to have a sister-in-law and I've never even met her. I mean, he hasn't even seen Dan or Paul since they were toddlers."

"Do your parents know?"

"No. They don't talk. I know they aren't going to let me go to the wedding."

"When is it?"

"December."

"Why didn't you tell me? This is awesome news."

"I didn't want to tell you online last night and then you came over and kissed me. I missed it so much I didn't want to stop you."

I take her hand and kiss it. "You should go anyway," I say.

"What do you mean?"

"You should go to your brother's wedding. It's his freaking wedding! You have to be there."

"My parents will never let me."

"Then don't tell them."

"You want me to lie to my parents and find some way to get to Denver on my own?"

"No, I want us to do it. If I'm invited that is."

"Oh my gosh!" she squeals. "You'll help me get there?"

"I will."

"Then yes! Yes! I can't believe I'm saying yes, but you're right. It's his wedding. What kind of sister would I be if I wasn't there?"

"A terrible sister. And I'd be a terrible boyfriend if I didn't get you there."

"We're going!"

"We're going."

Tess hugs me so tight I feel my back crack and then kisses me harder than ever before. Being a good guy has its perks.

Chapter 17

FRIENDS SHOW UP

That night while I'm researching how the hell we're going to get to Michael's wedding on public transportation, I get a call from James.

"Hey, man. What's up?" I say.

"I'm at the hospital."

"What happened?"

"My mom passed out and stopped breathing."

"Is she okay?"

"I don't know."

He sounds totally beat down. His voice is quiet and lifeless.

"What can I do?" I ask.

"Can I crash at your place tonight?"

"Yeah sure. You know what? I'll be there in twenty."

I hang up the phone and yell downstairs like a maniac. "Mom, get the car keys!"

I have my shoes and coat on by the time I get downstairs. She looks at me like I'm on something.

"James's mom is in the hospital. She's an alcoholic and James said she passed out and stopped breathing."

"Oh my god."

"I told James I'd be at the hospital."

She gets up and puts on her coat, grabs the keys, and we rush to the car.

We drive in silence. About halfway there I say, "I told him he could crash at our place tonight."

"Of course. Whatever he needs."

"Thanks Mom. I mean, thanks. Really. For not being like her."

She keeps her eyes on the road but smiles a little sadly.

When we get to the hospital, the elevator takes too long, so I leave my mom waiting for it and run up the stairs, taking three or four steps at a time.

When I get to the top and open the door, I see James sitting in the waiting room by himself. He's kicking his feet against the wall as he swings them back and forth.

"How is she?" I ask.

"She'll be okay. The doctors want to check her liver and some other stuff. She'll be here a few days."

"My mom said it's fine for you to stay with us."

He nods and I sit next to him. I don't know if I should put my hand on his shoulder or something comforting like that.

My mom comes out of the elevator, speed walks over to James, leans down and gives him a hug. She doesn't let go. She just kneels down and holds him.

I hear James sniffle. He buries his head into her shoulder while she strokes his back. His shoulders are moving up and he's crying. I put my hand on his back and we all just stay there like that until James has let it all out.

Chapter 18

A TEMPORARY BROTHER

James sleeps in Pete's room. I even tell him about the magazines under the mattress to cheer him up. Pete wouldn't mind.

In the morning, Dad makes us a big breakfast. Pancakes with strawberries and real syrup from Vermont. James has only ever had the corn syrup crap before.

"Have you heard any news about your mom this morning?" my Mom asks.

"She's doing better. She's awake and everything. I can go see her after school."

"How about we all go together?" she asks.

He looks at me for a second as if her question is funny.

"Thanks. I can take the bus though if you're busy."

"Nonsense. I'll pick you boys up after school."

"Thanks," he says.

We get ready and hop in the car so my dad can drop us off at school. As we're getting out of the car he hands James a bag. James gives him a questioning look.

"Lunch," Dad says with a smile. "Have a good day, boys."

He drives off and James and I walk toward the front building.

"Dude," says James.

"What?"

"Your parents are like, parents."

"Yeah."

"I mean even when my dad was alive we never had pancakes or bagged lunches. He was always busy working."

"We don't have pancakes every morning. Tomorrow will be cold cereal."

"Do you have milk in the house, which hasn't gone sour, that you didn't have to go out and buy yourself?"

"Yeah."

"Then it's better than my house."

"You know, maybe if your mom agrees to get some help, she'd let you stay with us for a while. I know my parents wouldn't mind."

"She's gotten help before."

"Maybe this time it will be different. I mean, she almost died."

"Maybe," he says, sounding unconvinced. "She's actually a pretty decent mom when she's sober. She doesn't make me lunch for school or anything. She'll cook dinner sometimes, and she bought me candy and stuff."

During lunch, James calls the hospital to check in.

"I don't remember the last time I talked to her when she was dry," he says, after getting off the phone.

"Dry?"

"Sober."

"Oh. Is she different?"

"She used to be angry. Now she sounds sad."

James doesn't really look at me when he says that. I want to say something that could help or make him feel better, but what do you say? It's not like it was an accident. She drank herself into the hospital. What kind of a person does that?

"You deserve better, man. You really do."

"She can be great," says James, still not looking at me.

"Great? She almost killed herself by drinking. If she would just stop, you could have a mom and she wouldn't be in the hospital."

"She's an alcoholic."

"And if she wasn't so selfish, she'd give it up. For you."

"Listen," he says angrily. "It's awesome that you have two parents who take care of you and siblings that you can talk to. I mean, what a freaking life. Your biggest problem is where you can make out with your girlfriend. My mom has real problems. So just back off, okay?"

I feel like a total d-bag. I don't know what to say so I just stand there feeling stupid.

"I know," says James, saving me from having to say anything. "You're a fricking Cosby kid. Even though my mom sucks at being a mom most of the time, it doesn't mean I hate her or anything. She's my mom."

"Yeah. Okay."

"I can still talk crap about her for the record. 'Cause she's my mom."

With that I pull a Seth and punch him in the arm.

At lunch Tess stops by the library on her way to meet her friends. I tell her what happened and ask if she wants to come to the hospital with us after school.

She calls her parents to see if she can go, but they say no. They know James is my friend and won't let her go anyplace where I'll be.

"They send their prayers for your mom, James."

"Well that's freaking helpful," I say.

Tess scowls at me. "You're becoming way more annoying about religion than when you first moved here. Just remember, your *girlfriend* is religious."

"It's okay," says James. "My mom would actually appreciate the prayers."

"I think I'll sit with you guys for lunch."

"Don't you have to meet your friends?" I ask, smiling to offset my jerkiness.

"I'm with my friends. Even if one of them is sometimes an idiot," she says, looking at me half smiling, half shaking her head.

After school, my mom and dad pick us up. We go straight to the hospital and stand in the waiting room while James goes in to see his mom.

I take out my homework and read some stuff for class, but I'm only half paying attention. I keep looking up the hallway waiting for him to come back.

About twenty minutes later he comes out and sits down next to us.

"How is she?" asks my mom.

"She's okay. She looks bad but the doctor told her she'd be fine. She just needs to stop drinking or she's going to bust her liver. And alcoholics don't get new ones."

We're all silent.

"There's something else," James says and takes a breath. "Child Protective Services came by to see her. They aren't convinced she can take care of me right now. Plus, she needs to go to rehab. I don't have any other family within like a hundred miles. So, I don't really know what to do."

James's voice is holding steady, but he's looking at the ground.

I look at my mom and dad and they nod.

"You can stay with us," I say. "I mean if your mom gives permission they have to let you, right?"

"Yes, of course, dear," says Mom. "You can stay with us for as long as you need. We'd love to have you."

James looks at her and then at me, and to save him from having to say anything, I say, "We'll watch movies in Pete's room."

"Want to come meet her?" he asks.

"We'd love to," Mom says.

Mrs. Bullard is hooked up to a clear liquid bag and her face looks like someone painted it gray and then gave her two black eyes.

"Mom, this is Ben. And this is his mom and dad. They said I could stay with them for a while so you could get better."

She nods, smiling and also sort of half crying. She takes my mom's hand and says, "Thank you. They want to take James away. But he's my boy. What will his dad think looking down on us if I lost him?"

"It's okay, Mom," James says. "You just have to get better. For real this time."

She nods. "This time I'll do it. I'll make you proud."

There is a moment of silence.

"Do you need anything from home?" my mom asks. "We could go get some of your things."

"You're so kind. I don't need anything. Would you be able to talk to the woman from Child Services though? I told her James would be coming back after school. She should be here."

"Let me go find out," says Dad.

When he comes back in the room, he's with an older woman wearing a suit. My mom puts out her hand, introduces herself, and says, "James is best friends with my son Ben. We'd love to have him stay with us as long as he needs to."

"These are good people," says James's mom. "They took him in last night and Ben is the only real friend James has. Please let him stay with them," she says.

The woman nods formally. "Mr. and Mrs. Pinter, if you could come with me so I can ask you a few questions about your residence," she says.

"Yes, of course," says my mom and follows her out of the room.

Chapter 19

IF YOU SEE YOUR GIRLFRIEND'S SISTER'S BOOBS, LOOK AWAY. NOW.

H aving James live with me is even better than I expected. We get our homework done in half the time, which is great because it leaves more time for watching movies, reading comics, and hanging out.

James also visits his mom a lot in rehab. She has to be there for a month or so. Living here is probably the most normal family experience he's ever had.

Three days a week at school, during our free period, Tess and I meet in the auditorium in our spot. This goes on pretty flawlessly for two weeks. And because James is an awesome guy who feels like he owes me one, he hangs out in the seats in the auditorium and acts as lookout, just in case someone does come in.

Everything is going great. In fact, life is better than it's ever freaking been before. I'm living with my best friend. I get to see my girlfriend. James's mom is getting better. And because she isn't around, for the first time in his life he doesn't have to go to church.

Like I said, everything is perfect. Until one day during our auditorium time Tess has to go to the bathroom. We walk out of the costume room together. That is the first big mistake. Then we walk past the green room. Because the light is on in there, we look inside. That is the second big mistake.

Inside, I see Angela half naked and making out with some senior. Tess looks over and is so surprised that she drops her bag and gasps. Yep, she actually gasps.

Angela covers herself and turns around in time to see my face and Tess's face staring at her.

Tess doesn't even hesitate. She opens the door and yells, "Put your clothes on right now."

I stay outside the room. A few seconds later the senior, still putting his shirt back on, strides out of the room.

"Hey," he says as he walks by.

"Oh, um, hey," I say.

He puts his bag over his shoulder and jumps down off the stage to leave.

"What is wrong with you?" I hear Tess say.

"What's wrong with me? I'm not the one hanging out with him," she says, pointing at me, "against orders from Mom and Dad."

"Yeah, well, I'm not the one taking my clothes off for some guy just because he's on the football team. I mean, he's not even your boyfriend."

It goes on like that for a while, both of them threatening to tell their parents. I'm trying to get the image of Angela's naked upper half out of my head. It's got to be against some boyfriend code to know what your girlfriend's sister looks like naked. I don't even know what Tess looks like that naked.

Now that I think about it, this is probably how Trent knew that the auditorium was empty during the day. Angela probably brought him here.

James comes running backstage.

He says, "I'm sorry. I had to take a leak. I didn't see her come in."

I tune back in to hear Angela say, "I can do whatever I want. Back off."

"Then why can't I do what I want? Why are you so against me hanging out with Ben?"

"You may not like what I was doing with John, but he's a Christian. I wonder what Mom and Dad will care about more. Me with him or you with your sinner."

I get up and walk into the room.

"Hey, Angela. You may think I'm a terrible person because I'm an atheist, but me and your sister have never done the things you were doing with that guy."

"You arrogant little—"

"Watch your language," I say smiling. "God is watching."

Angela grabs her backpack and leaves, slamming the auditorium door as she goes.

Tess turns to me looking shaken. "She can't tell. She knows that she'd get in trouble too," I say to her.

"Not as much trouble as me."

"So you're telling me that your parents would be more pissed at you for seeing me than they would be at your sister for mounting the nearest football player she could find."

"We'll see," says Tess.

She steps away from me and gives me a weird look.

"What?" I ask.

"Did you see?"

"See what?" I ask uncomfortably.

"My sister without her clothes on."

"Maybe," I say with a cringe.

"Great."

"It's not like . . ."

"Not like what? She's gorgeous."

"You're gorgeous." I reach out to her but she brushes me off. "You won't hug me?"

"You won't be thinking of me."

"Just because I saw her doesn't mean I want her. I want you."

Tess won't look at me and she starts to cry a little.

"What's wrong?"

"I hate her so much. And now you've seen her and we haven't even . . ."

"Stop. Okay? Just stop. I think you're beautiful and you're also a wonderful person. And when you're ready to do more, we'll do more. Okay?"

"You don't wish you were with her?" she says with tears on her cheeks.

"I think I hate her even more than you do."

"Promise?"

"Promise. I'm not saying I wouldn't want to see you like that. I mean, I really really really . . ."

"Stop talking," she says, half laughing between tears.

"Done."

Chapter 20

WHEN A BAD DAY GETS WORSE

After getting caught with Tess by Angela, the last thing I want to do is go to biology and listen to Mr. Thompson go on and on about the importance of the Bible in science. But that's what's next.

For the first time since my new straight-A goal I'm having a hard time listening. I never raise my hand anymore in this class. Not since he was such a jerk about that blood thing. At least we aren't talking about the circulatory system any more. It's the respiratory system now. Not that I'm even really paying attention. I'm just worried Angela is going to tell her parents. Even if she doesn't, Angela seeing me and Tess in the auditorium means we can't use it as a hiding spot anymore. Which means we have no place to hang out. Again.

"Ben?" Mr. Thompson says.

"Um, yeah?"

"Did you hear me?"

"No. I guess I . . ."

He sighs. "I asked if you could tell me how it came to be that man breathed his first breath."

"I don't know."

"You don't know?"

"I mean, that happened millions of years ago before man was even man. No one knows I don't think."

The class laughs. Mr. Thompson doesn't look amused.

"Every other student in the class knows this Ben. Just not you."

"Is it some Bible thing?" I ask with more attitude than usual.

"Open up your textbook to the chapter on the respiratory system and read the first sentence, please," he says.

"And the Lord God formed man of the dust of the ground, and breathed into his nostrils the breath of life; and man became a living soul." I close the book.

"So I ask again, please tell me how it came to be that man breathed his first breath?"

"My answer hasn't changed."

No one in the class is laughing now. Mr. Thompson is starting to look really annoyed.

"And what about the Creator? Would you just ignore Him?"

I pause for a second, trying to decide how to answer him. I didn't lie to Tess's parents so why lie now?

"I don't believe in a creator," I say. "I believe in evolution. No one gave us a respiratory system. We developed it over millions of years."

Mr. Thompson takes his glasses off and puts them on his desk. Kenny makes a chimp noise and throws a wadded up piece of paper at me. Tess's friend Beth gives him a dirty look.

Mr. Thompson turns to Kenny and says, "We have a student in class who, if he died tomorrow, would go to hell. You think that's funny Mr. Schrock?"

Kenny looks down at his desk. "No sir."

"Then I suggest you keep quiet."

Mr. Thompson turns his attention back to me and says, "Stay after class. I want to talk to you."

When the bell rings I get my stuff together and wait in my seat until the other kids are gone. Then I go up to Mr. Thompson's desk.

I just stand there while he puts his notes in order. He looks up at me and smiles.

"Yes, Ben. Thank you for staying."

He looks at me, his fat lips tight and moving between a smile and a frown before he actually starts speaking.

"You've got a remarkable scientific mind. You pay attention to details and you seem to really have a knack for biology and understanding the mechanics of how things work. With that said, that's only a portion of this class." He leans forward and looks me straight in the eyes. "How we apply science is equally important. I need to know that you're able to take what you've learned and put it in context with the Bible and the teachings of our Lord Jesus Christ. Do you understand?"

"Your lord Jesus Christ," is all I can manage to say under my breath.

Mr. Thompson leans back in his chair and says, "You've been here for a month and a half now. More than enough time to start your journey toward Christ. Perhaps you haven't looked into the subject deeply enough. I want you to write me a two-page paper on why knowing the facts isn't enough. Why a good scientific mind also has to have a background in the Bible. Due next Friday."

What I really want to say is, *I hate you and this*

entire school for trying to change my beliefs. All that comes out of my mouth is, "Seriously?"

"You're a great student and I want to see you excel. This is about more than just a grade. Although your grade will suffer if you don't do it. More important, it's about your soul. Get it done."

I hesitate for a second, then just say, "Yes sir." What else am I supposed to say?

"Good boy. See you tomorrow."

Chapter 21

CHRISTIAN RULE #87: DATING AN ATHEIST IS WORSE THAN DRY HUMPING A GUY YOU AREN'T DATING.

That night I text Tess but she doesn't respond. I email her too but still nada. I don't even see the light on in her room. I have no idea just how much trouble she's in for seeing me.

Tess isn't at school the next day. Angela is. And any chance she gets she looks over at me and smirks. She does it so many times that I have no choice but to start pretending to lift up my shirt. I realize that it's immature and mean. It also shuts her up fast.

During lunch when James and I are in the library I see Beth walk by a few times. She looks at me and then turns away. As far as I know Beth doesn't know that Tess and I are a thing, but then why would she be hovering?

So I wave and say, "Hey, Beth."

"Hey," she says, and for a moment it looks like she

might say something else. Then she walks out of the library.

"Should I go after her?" asks James. "She might know where Tess is."

I shake my head. "Not a good idea."

I want to ask her what's up with Tess but it could just make things worse. I do the next best thing. After school when James and I get home I ask him to call her.

"What do you want me to say?"

"Just pretend to be her lab partner. I think his name is Dean.

"I don't sound like Dean."

"Her parents don't know that. Just trust me."

He shakes his head, picks up his phone, and dials Tess's home number.

"Hi, this is Dean. Is Tess there? Oh, I'm calling because she's my lab partner and she didn't tell me she was sick today or anything. Oh, is everything okay? Oh. Okay. I understand. Thanks." James hangs up.

"So?" I say.

"She's at church dealing with family problems."

"Meaning she's the problem?"

"Probably."

"So she's the problem and her sister just gets a pass!"

"It sucks."

"Understatement of the year."

"Have you ever thought . . ."

"What?"

"I know it sucks, but have you ever thought about cooling it with Tess? I mean, a secret relationship in this town is almost impossible."

"Her parents are the ones who are wrong. Not me."

"Tess is getting in trouble. Like big trouble."

"James," my dad calls from downstairs. "Did you still want to go visit your mom? I'm ready."

"You'll figure it out," James says to me. "Gotta go. Mom freaks out if she doesn't see me for a few days in a row."

James and my dad leave. Now that I'm alone I try to think of a way for Tess and me to keep seeing each other. It wouldn't be much of a relationship if we never got to hang out.

I need a grown-up opinion. But not my parents. And James has never even had a girlfriend. I do the only thing I can think of. I write to Pete.

Pete,

I know you're in the middle of the desert and have way more important things to do than give your little brother advice, but I need your help.

School is going better since James and I started hanging out. He's staying in your room while his mom is in rehab. And I have a girl-friend. Her name is Tess and she's awesome. The problem is that technically we're not allowed to see each other. Her family is really religious and once they found out I was an atheist, they told her she's not allowed to see me. We've been sneaking around. First outside at night (she lives across the street) but Dad caught us. Then we found a place to hang out during lunch at school, but her evil older sister caught us and ratted to her parents. She's in so much trouble she wasn't even at school today.

So what do I do? How do I get around the

parental blockades? It's not right that her parents hate me so much.

Ben

I don't know if there is a temporary truce happening in the war zone or if the guys are having a barbeque, but two hours later Pete writes back.

Ben,

Are you stupid? Do you really have no idea how to sneak away and spend some time with your girl? Since you're essentially failing at what it means to be a teenager, here is the simple fact: Both of you need to lie. It's normally not something I'd recommend. And if you ever show this to Mom I will shave your head while you're sleeping . . . and we all remember what a dumb-looking, square head you've got.

Have Tess tell her parents she's doing something with her friends. You do the same if Mom and Dad know that her parents forbid you guys from seeing each other. And then get together. If you have a friend who is willing to cover for you if a parent calls then all the better.

DON'T DO IT TOO OFTEN. And change up the days and the lies each time.

Good luck.

Pete

Aside from the insults it's a really good suggestion. I don't know why we haven't thought of it. I text Tess again.

"We're idiots."

She responds right away. "Why?"

"I asked my bro how we can see each other without getting in trouble and he pointed out that we're stupid."

"He has a way?!"

"Yes. But it involves lying. Are you cool with that?"

"I'm already lying. And I pretty much hate my parents right now."

"Tell your parents you're hanging out with a friend and I tell my parents I'm hanging out with a friend. Then we hang out together instead."

"Where do we go?"

"Some place where none of your friends or family would ever be caught dead. A secular movie or something?"

"I'm grounded."

"I figured. But they can't lock you up forever."

"I miss you."

"I miss you too."

"Only problem is none of my friends know about you. And my parents will see their parents at church. If I lie they might find out."

"You should tell Beth. She's your best friend. She should know."

"What if she freaks . . ."

"I don't think she will. I think she tried to talk to me today."

"She's asked me about you a few times. I've lied and I hate it."

"We need to trust someone. She's our best bet."

"I know."

"You're amazing."

"I'm scared! L"

"It will be okay. Promise."

"<3"

Chapter 22

REQUIREMENT: BEST FRIENDS MUST BE AWESOME

Tess is back at school the next day. She avoids looking at me when we pass in the hall. When I go to my locker before lunch there is a note inside.

It says: I wish I could kiss your face. I'm talking to Beth at lunch. Keep your fingers crossed!

If Beth doesn't say yes, Tess is going to feel even worse. Not only will her family be against her. Her best friend will be too. James and I hang out at lunch and during study hall. Still no word. Nothing in my locker and no texts.

At the end of the day on my way to talent show rehearsal the hallways are almost empty. I turn a corner and suddenly see Kenny walking toward me.

"Hey fag," he says, smirking. "How are you and your boyfriend doing? His mom dead yet?"

"You know I'm not actually gay, right? I mean there's nothing wrong with gay people but I'm straight."

He walks right up to my face and says, "It almost

doesn't matter. Straight or queer you're still going to hell. Just where you belong."

"Seriously, man. What's your problem?"

"This is a Christian country and a Christian school. You don't deserve to be in either."

"Says you," I say as I try to walk away.

Kenny steps toward me and blocks my way. "Everyone here wants you gone. How does it feel to be hated? Hated so much that someone might just do something about it one day."

I want to make a smart-ass remark in response, but I'm actually a little scared of him now. It's probably a bad idea to taunt a kid who is bigger than you and who hates you. So I turn around and walk away. When I look behind me Kenny is gone. What an asshole. I breathe deep, glad that he didn't actually punch me this time. When I get to rehearsal my heart is still racing. Tess is already inside. She doesn't even look my way. Not a hint. Not even a wink. Does that mean it went badly with Beth? Is she mad at me?

I sort of practice my magic act but I'm too distracted to do it right so my reveals are lazy. I keep looking over at Tess. She's just talking to a girl from the drama group, laughing like nothing happened.

Finally, people start to leave. I take my time and tell Trent I need to stay and work on my act more. Tess leaves too but doesn't take her jacket. About five minutes later the door opens again.

"Hey!" I say, running up to her and hugging her.

"Hey," says a voice that doesn't belong to Tess.

I let go of Tess and look behind her. It's Beth.

"So you're the reason perfect Tess has betrayed her family and ditched her friends?"

"No! I mean, it's not like that."

"Relax," she says. "I'm only messing with you."

"So you're cool with it?"

"My sister married a Jewish guy. My parents weren't happy at first. They got over it. Well, at least enough to see them once in a while. Tess says you're good to her and I trust her. More than she trusts me apparently."

I walk up and hug her. She gives me an awkward pat on the back.

"Too much?" I say to Tess.

"Maybe a little."

"It's nice to have more than two people in the entire school who care. And who don't want to beat me up."

"If little Ms. Paranoid had confided in her best friend sooner, you might not be in this mess," Beth says a little harshly.

Tess hugs Beth tightly and pleads. "I'm sorry. How many times can I say I'm sorry to make you believe me?" Beth shakes her head with a smile and hugs her back.

Suddenly Tess turns to me. "Wait, who wants to beat you up?"

"Kenny just threatened me in the hall. He's all talk, he didn't make a move or anything."

Tess looks concerned. Then she shakes her head. "He wouldn't actually do anything. He'd get into too much trouble. Right?"

"Yeah, of course. Forget it," I say, thinking about how he wrote fag on my locker.

Beth turns to me. "You know, I've been asking her for weeks if you two are a thing. And she lied. Lied and lied and lied again. I mean, the first week of school you guys were hanging out all the time, and then it was like, nothing. She would disappear at lunch and take forever to answer her texts. It all makes sense now."

"It's not totally her fault," I say quickly. "If I had just lied to her parents originally then none of this would have happened."

"I guess you guys can't be together without lying to someone. I'm just glad it's not me anymore."

"Me too," says Tess as she takes Beth's hand. "I hated it."

"So what now?" says Beth. "I mean, you guys told me for a reason, right? And not just because Tess's parents think she's on a path to the devil?"

"We can't see each other," I say.

"How does that bring me into it?" she asks.

Tess says, "My parents know we hang out all the time. Maybe sometimes I could tell them that we're together, but you know, see Ben instead."

"You want me to lie?"

"How about we don't lie?" I say. "How about me, you, Beth and James all hang out together? Then no one is lying. We're all with who we said we were with, and we still get to see each other."

"Not like a double date," says Beth. "I mean, he's a freshman."

"Not a double date," I say. "Although James is a good guy."

"You could do worse," says Tess, smiling.

"You might not mind dating an atheist but I like my guys heaven-bound," she says, smirking at me.

"See, if you were me you wouldn't care because you'd think we're all just going to end up as worm food anyway," I say smiling.

"Ew," she says.

"There is one other time that might require a lie," I say.

"When?" asks Tess.

"Your brother's wedding."

"Your brother is getting married?!" asks Beth. "You didn't tell me that!"

"We could all go to the wedding," Tess says. "I just have no idea how we'll get there."

And then it comes to me. I'm so stupid for not thinking of it before.

"My brother will take us," I say. "He'll be home and I know he'll do it."

Tess looks at Beth and says, "I know I'm asking a lot. And I understand if you don't want to lie."

"Like Ben said, I won't be lying. I'll be hanging out with you. I just won't mention the other people."

"I'm sorry I didn't trust you."

"I've always been there for you and I always will be."

Chapter 23

IS THE DEFINITION OF INSANITY DOING THE SAME THING OVER AND OVER WHILE EXPECTING A DIFFERENT RESULT?

t's the night before my science paper is due and I haven't written a word. I'm two weeks ahead on my homework in all my other classes, but this stupid paper is killing me. I've even been doing research on evolution versus creation. On anything at all the Bible says that could relate to the stuff we're learning about now. Nothing. Zip. And I'm supposed to write a paper anyway. How does stuff written a few thousand years ago have anything to do with what we know now? Why can't religion and science just be kept separate?

Tess has fed me a bunch of verses I could use. I'm lucky her parents didn't take away her computer when they grounded her. She even sent me underlined passages from her textbook, but the textbook is just wrong, so how can I use it?

They want me to learn stuff that goes along with the

Bible instead of the stuff that there's actual evidence for. I know it's a Christian school but we should still learn about the theories that have actual proof to back them up.

Maybe they worry that if people believe in science, they won't believe in god. People can believe in both. Tess does.

I start writing twelve or more times, but each time I want to say how it's all bull and how Thompson should let me stick to the science. So I start over. I write a paper on why I think it's important to let me concentrate just on the facts. I have science on my side. They've got an old book where god kills way more people than Satan ever did. Probably shouldn't put that in the essay unless I want to fail. Really, knowing the science alone should be enough to get me a good grade.

It turns into a five-page paper. I read it over and take out anything that could be seen as not respecting his religion. I try to make clear that I hope he respects my beliefs the way I respect his.

I get a text from Tess asking to read it.

I respond, "I don't think you want to."

"Why not?"

"Because I told the truth."

"Come on, you know what he wants. Just say it."

"Why should I have to lie about who I am?"

"Because right now lying will help you. Kind of like lying to my parents is the best for us right now."

"Funny that the good Christian girl wants me to lie."

"Just because I'm Christian doesn't mean I'm perfect."

"You seem pretty perfect to me."

"Don't change the subject. Thompson is going to be furious."

"He can't force me to believe something I don't."

"He can give you a bad grade."

"I'm one of the best students he has."

"You're being stubborn. Don't you think you're just asking for trouble now? Why can't you just suck it up and say what he wants to hear for once?"

"I've thought about it and I don't want to lie about who I am and what I think."

"Must be nice to have the choice to be yourself. If I told the truth I'd probably get kicked out of my house."

"I never said that you should tell your parents the truth."

"You think I'm a coward because I haven't."

"Where did you get that? I don't think you're a coward."

Nothing. No response.

"Are you mad at me now?" I text.

Still no response.

Maybe she's pissed that I won't lie while she has to. But I won't lose my family for standing up for my beliefs. She has to know it's different. Crap.

Chapter 24

HANDING IN A COUPLE PAGES OF TRUTH

When I get to school the next day Tess is sitting near my locker.

She waits for the bell to ring and even though I don't think Tess has ever even been late to a class, she doesn't get up. She just watches the last few kids scramble into their classes.

I finally turn to her and ask, "What's wrong?"

"Did you fix your paper?" She asks a little angrily.

"It didn't need to be fixed."

"Who cares if you don't tell Mr. Thompson the truth? You know what he wants to hear. I worked my butt off sending you quotes to use. And you just blow it off like it's nothing!"

"Why are you so bent on this? It's my decision."

"Because I know when you get that paper back you're going to be mad at yourself and mad at Mr. Thompson, and it's going to make things worse. Just tell him what he wants to hear. It really doesn't matter. He's not your family. He's not your friend. His opinion doesn't matter. Get a good grade and be done. You know that science and the Bible don't fit together. Knowing that should be enough. It's like you want to take every opportunity possible to tell people that you think the Bible is stupid. So take this. It's a two-page paper I wrote last night that will get Mr. Thompson off your back."

"You wrote me a paper?"

"You can thank me later."

"You're the best girlfriend ever," I say.

"I know. Here, take it."

"I can't."

"Are you kidding me?"

"It's not your grade, Tess. It's mine. And I don't want to get it by lying. That's not throwing it in his face. That's telling the truth."

"But I'm a great liar, huh?" she says, dropping the paper to the floor.

"That's not what I said."

"You think I don't want to tell the truth too? Like it's fun for me to lie to my family and sneak around? It's hard and it sucks. I do it because I want to be with you."

"I'd lie to be with you too."

"You wouldn't lie to my parents."

"You're bringing that up again?"

"Our whole relationship would have been so easy if you could have just said you believed in God. Or were interested in learning about it. Faked it. For me. You can't even do it for a stupid paper?"

"I know it sucks for you to lie to your family. If you didn't you could get kicked out of your house. It's serious for you. For me it's a choice."

"If you had lied, my life would have been so much easier. Did you think of that?"

"I thought your parents would be reasonable. If I could go back maybe I would lie. I never meant to make life hard for you. I just want to be with you and be who I am."

Tess crumbles and suddenly starts crying. I put my arm around her and she buries her head in my chest and sobs. Even though we just had a fight and she's crying, it still feels awesome to say screw it and talk to each other in school.

"I'm sorry," I say.

"But you're still going to turn in that stupid paper, aren't you?"

"Yeah," I say, kind of scared she's going to start yelling again.

"You are such an idiot," she says, exhausted.

"He can't give me a bad grade. I used freaking citations on this mother. He can't say I didn't research it and give a good argument."

"We should go to class," she says.

"Just a few more minutes, okay?"

"Okay."

"I really didn't mean to make your life harder. You're the best person I know. And the bravest," I say.

"I just wish it was all easier. You're the best thing that's happened to me. I just can't lose my family."

"Do you want to stop seeing each other?"

She pauses. My hearts quickens. I didn't think she'd pause. I thought she'd immediately say *no, that's stupid*. But she's silent.

"Tess?"

"Sometimes I think maybe we should stop."

"Is that what you want?"

"No."

"Me neither."

"I'm just tired of it being this hard."

"What could I do to make it easier?"

"Just always be there for me okay? I need someone on my side."

I kiss her forehead. "I'm here."

Chapter 25

FRIENDS HELP FRIENDS DO LAUNDRY

For the next week, James and I just hang out at home, do our homework, and visit his mom in rehab. The doctor says she's doing really well. James says that's happened before.

"I don't want to go back," he says.

"Why?" I ask. Although it seems like a stupid question. Here he gets cooked meals, his laundry done, help with homework, and responsible adults who can get him to school on time.

"She's been sober for a few weeks before. Even three months once. But she's been an alcoholic since before my dad died. It just got worse after that."

"You know how to handle yourself."

"It's not just me having to handle myself. We're in the system now. Child Services is going to check on us to make sure she's not a mess. I don't think she can do it."

"What would they do if she started drinking again?"

"They could put me in foster care."

"Maybe this time she'll really beat it. I mean, the doctors said it was serious, right?"

"If she keeps drinking she'll need a new liver. And they won't give a liver transplant to an alcoholic who failed rehab this many times. And I think you need to be clean for a year or two to even qualify for one."

"She hasn't failed this time," I say.

"No one can fail while they're in rehab. It's right after, when they can't freaking handle the real world. I wish she could just stay there. She's more of a mom right now than she's ever been at home."

We sit there not saying anything. James looks like he's thinking hard. Like he might cry or punch something. Then he says, "I never thought I could actually be better if I got taken away from my mom. Maybe I'd end up some place like this. Hot meals. A clean house. Someone who doesn't drink herself to freaking death."

I just sit there not saying anything, because what do you say? Nothing. There is absolutely zero that I could say that would mean anything. For Tess and for James I'm useless. And then it hits me.

"I have an idea. We're going to your house."

"Why?"

"Just trust me."

I grab my bike and James grabs Pete's old bike and we ride to his house. It's only a few miles, but James kind of drags behind me.

When we get there James parks the bike and stands in front of the door.

"So really, why are we here?" he asks.

"Just go in," I say.

"It's just . . ."

"Come on. We're here."

It takes him a second before he opens the door and walks in.

It's my first time in his house. Now I know why he didn't want me to see it. There is stuff everywhere. Liquor bottles. Clothes. Food.

James goes right over to the window and opens it to get rid of some of the smell. I can feel him looking at me so I try not to react.

"It's disgusting, isn't it?" says James. "She's usually too out of it to notice the mess and I got tired of cleaning up after her."

He starts picking up some paper plates with crusts and junk still on them and throws them in the garbage.

"So why did you want to come here?" he asks. "To make me more depressed?"

"I just thought we could get rid of the liquor in the house so the place would be okay for your mom to come back to. No temptations, you know?"

"Yeah, okay" he says, relaxing a bit.

I grab the bottles on the kitchen counter and the table. Empty beer bottles, vodka bottles, boxed wine, and some other stuff I don't recognize.

James goes into the cupboards, under his mom's bed, behind the couch and even under the sink in the bathroom to grab bottles by the handful. Most are empty. Some are half full.

He holds up a bottle of something brown and looks at it. I mean really stares the thing down. Then he opens it and drinks some straight from the bottle.

He screws up his face like he's just been fed rat pee and wipes his mouth.

I don't even have to say anything for him to know

that I think he's nuts. His mom is in rehab and he's drinking her booze? That's all kinds of messed up.

"Shouldn't I know what makes this crap more important than her own son? Hell, don't I deserve it?"

"You don't drink. You told me that."

He takes another gulp. This time when he pulls the bottle away from his mouth his eyes are wet.

"I don't drink," he says. He looks at the bottle. "It doesn't even taste good."

"So put it down."

"Try it."

I want to take the bottle. I want to try drinking it. I've never been drunk. But James looks so angry that I can't do it.

"We should be throwing this stuff out."

"We will," he says.

James sits down on the couch with the bottle.

"This is where she sits all day. I've never had friends over. She walks around . . . " James stops talking for a second and takes another drink. "She forgets to put on clothes. You know what that's like? To be in a house all the time with someone so freaking out of it? With a mom who can't even get dressed?"

"I'm sorry."

"Just sit down and have a drink. I've earned it."

"Only if you promise me this is the only drink you'll have. Once you're done we'll clean up and throw all this crap out."

James takes another gulp and passes me the bottle. I tip it toward my mouth. The second it hits the back of my throat I almost puke it back up.

"That's freaking disgusting," I say, now knowing why James was gasping for air before.

"It gets less bad the more you drink."

I hold on to the bottle so that James can't have anymore. We just sit there not saying anything for what seems like forever.

"I hate her."

"She has a problem. An addiction."

"It's like she can't stand being sober. When she's clean she looks even more scared than when she's drunk. Like making dinner is some big impossible thing to do. I hope she fails."

"Dude."

"It's true. Then I could get out of here."

James is starting to look kind of dazed. He doesn't even ask for the bottle back. He just sits there looking mad.

"Are you drunk?" I ask.

"Maybe. I've never been drunk before."

"How does it feel?"

"Kind of like I want to cry, punch my mom in the face, and go to sleep."

"Why don't you break something?"

"Like what?"

"This," I say, handing him the bottle.

"Break it?" he says with a hiccup.

"Smash it."

James grabs the bottle and stands up, maybe a bit too fast because he sways a bit.

"Get me the trash can from the garage."

I run out and grab the biggest trashcan out there and bring it back.

James stands in front of it, takes another drink from the bottle, then looks at the booze with more hatred than I've ever seen on anyone's face.

"Do it," I say, putting my hand on his shoulder.

Like he just woke up, he raises the bottle over his head with two hands and smashes it down into the bottom of the can. As soon as I hear the sound I slam the lid down to stop glass shards from flying out. James grabs more bottles from the kitchen. He smashes bottle after bottle, hurling them as hard as he can, getting more pissed off with each one. I try to cover the trash as best I can, but suddenly he lets out a small shout of pain and holds his arm.

"What happened?"

"Glass," he says, holding his hand over a small gash on his forearm. "And I think I might puke."

I bring him over to the bathroom where he slumps down on the tile. He holds out his arm, not even looking at it.

"It's not bad. Just a cut. You have Band-Aids?"

"Of course not."

I grab some toilet paper and say, "Hold this on it."

James stares off into space but does what I tell him.

"I thought this was supposed to make stuff better," he says. "I thought drinking made a person less sad or made them forget the crap they have to deal with. It doesn't. It's worse. So why does she do it?"

"I don't know." He's silent. "You stay here, okay? I'm going to clean up."

James doesn't say anything. From the looks of it he's going to cry, and he's waiting for me to leave so I don't see him. So I go.

I start with the rest of the bottles. I find more under the sink, behind the bed, and in the laundry room. I empty them all and chuck them in the recycling. Then I start doing something I've never really done in my own house. Cleaning up. I grab dirty clothes and put them by the washing machine. I straighten the pillows on the couch and clean the dishes in the sink. I throw out old food from the refrigerator. I even vacuum.

Once the living room is finished, I open a door to a room neither of us has been in yet. It's James's room. And it's spotless. Seriously. The bed is made. Every pencil and pen is in a cup on the desk. Clothes are folded and put away. It looks like a grown-up's room. Definitely the opposite of mine.

Next to his bed is a picture of James and his dad at a park. James looks like he's only seven or eight years old.

"I don't let my mom in here," he says, walking up behind me.

James's eyes are bloodred, but he looks a bit better. More in control.

"It's a nice room," I say.

He hands me some detergent and says, "Mind starting the laundry?"

"Sure thing."

James grabs the vacuum and starts sucking up all the dirt on the floor. Some glass too from the broken bottles.

We spend three hours in almost total silence, both of us cleaning and taking it very seriously. James only stops once to throw up. He doesn't even look drunk now. Just determined.

When neither of us sees anything else that needs to be done, we sit on the couch and look around.

"Someone could actually live here now," he says.

"Have you ever drank any of this stuff before today?"

"No. Drinking is for losers," he says, half laughing. Not like he really thinks it's funny. It's dark. Really dark.

He looks over at the chair in the corner. "See that?" he says."

"Yeah."

"That's where she passed out and almost died."

"Come on," I say. "Tomorrow is garbage day. Let's bring this stuff out to the curb."

"Yeah. Okay."

Chapter 27

I STILL KNOW HOW TO CURSE

Tess and I have been texting and talking online every night, but it's just not the same. I hate missing someone who walks by me in the hall everyday. By Thursday I just want school to be over so James and I can go home, read some comics or watch a movie, and wait for Saturday to come. Me, Tess, James, and Beth are all hanging out together. The way it should be.

During study hall I leave a note in Tess's locker. I write, "Can't wait to see you." Tess would have drawn a smiley face or something on a note to me, but I think she'll get that I miss her.

Beth nods to me in the hallway now, which is a nice change. It's like I've got an actual group of friends. Even bigger than the group I had back at my old school. Of course I wasn't ignored by the other 99% of the population at my old school like I am here.

I think I'll ask Tess if she wants to sit in the back of the movie theater so if the movie is bad we can just make out. Hopefully it will be bad. Plus, I've been waiting to tell her that I emailed Pete and he's game for driving us to her brother's wedding. She's going to freak out.

In science class Mr. Thompson hands back a whole bunch of papers and tests. Flipping through my papers, I see nothing below an A-. Until I get to the bottom. My extra assignment on science and the Bible. There is a big fat F written at the top in thick red pen. F as in Fail. F as in, you've got to be effing kidding me.

Kenny is sitting next to me. He looks across at my paper and laughs hysterically, like my failing grade is the funniest thing he's ever seen in his life. A few other kids turn and look at me, chuckling as if they're all in on the joke.

"That's what you deserve, fag," Kenny mutters to me.

I feel my face get red and my hands hold the paper so tight that it's crumpling. I researched this stupid thing. I had evidence. People way smarter than Thompson backing me up.

I want to throw it in Mr. Thompson's face.

I want to kick my desk over and throw acid on the floor.

I want to take my stupid textbook and set it on fire.

Once class is dismissed I wait for everyone to clear out. Kenny is the last one to leave and laughs at me one more time before closing the door behind him. I sit totally still in my seat until Mr. Thompson notices me.

"Yes, Ben?"

"You gave me an F."

"I did."

"I had footnotes. You can think I'm wrong but are you going to tell me that the greatest scientists of the time are wrong too?"

"I told you exactly what I wanted from this paper,

Ben. I'm sorry that you feel it's unfair. But the paper is wrong. All of it. I can't give a passing grade on something like that."

"Can I ask how this is going to affect my grade?"

"I'm afraid it's going to affect it quite severely."

"How severely?"

"Well, let me see."

He takes out a calculator and his grade book and starts plugging in numbers like it's nothing at all. He finishes, shakes his head, and looks at me.

"That paper brought you down to a C+."

"You're telling me I went from an A to a C+ with one stupid paper?"

"I'm afraid so. And if you don't start incorporating biblical evidence into your papers, you're going to find that your grade will get even lower."

"I know the freaking science!"

"I think you'd better watch your language."

"Screw that! I'm the best student in this class and you want to bring my grade down to a C+ because of one paper on something that isn't even science? The Bible has nothing to do with science. They're just stories! Fiction! The only class we should be studying it in is English."

Mr. Thompson stands, his face red. "You attend a Christian school whether you like it or not and we teach the truth based not only on science but also on what the Bible, the word of God, the truth, teaches us. You're more than welcome to stay ignorant if that's what you want. In this class the Bible is science and you don't know the material. So yes, you get a C+. And if you keep up with this behavior I can't even guarantee that."

"Yeah well, we'll see about that."

I grab my stuff and walk to the door without looking back. All my work, and this religious nut is going to bring down my GPA. I open the door but instead of taking a first step into the hallway I trip over something big and, in what feels like less than a second, I'm falling face first, my feet still tangled in whatever I tripped over. I put my hands out to brace my fall but not fast enough. I twist my body trying to save my chin and nose from hitting the ground. It barely works. I fall down on my left arm and smack my cheek into the ground.

The hallway goes quiet. I don't move. I just lay there feeling like my face and shoulder have exploded. Then there is a hand on my back. James is saying, "Are you okay?" I'm too stunned to answer. I sit up and look back to see what tripped me. Kenny is leaning next to the door, his backpack is twisted around my ankles.

"You're pretty clumsy," says Kenny sneering.

"You tripped me!" I say angrily. I stand up, opening and closing my mouth to make sure my jaw is okay and lifting up my arm to make sure my shoulder still works.

"I guess sinners just aren't protected by God in the same way as everyone else."

James puts his hand on my shoulder. "We should go," he says. I shake him off.

Ignoring my pain, I walk right up to Kenny.

"You ignorant asshole. The fact that you really believe that means you're freaking stupid. Heaven doesn't exist and even if it did, none of your ignorant mean asses would be allowed in. You're only nice to the people who are exactly like you, and everything I've learned about Jesus says that he was nice to everyone."

By now there is a crowd of kids around us, all staring

silently at me. Kenny could probably beat the crap out of me right now and none of them would care enough to stop him.

"You're all freaking hypocrites," I say, not just to Kenny but to all of them. "Stupid small town Bible thumpers! The only thing I wish is that there really was an afterlife, because when you all die and nothing happens, I won't get to see the look on your face that there is nothing. That all your stupid beliefs and rules were pointless. God doesn't exist. And you're all too stupid to realize it."

Then before I can stop it, before I can think about how terrible what I'm saying is, I shout the F word. And not just the F word. I sandwich it between the two worst words I could ever choose. Clutching my hurt arm, I yell Jesus f***ing Christ at the top of my lungs. And for a second, it feels great. Like I've finally been able to say what I've been thinking since I got here. They might shun me, hate me, push me to the ground, and fail me, but here's what I really freaking think of all you.

Every single head within earshot turns toward me. Some look hurt. Most look mad. So mad that if it was physically possible smoke would be coming out of their ears. If they thought I was going to hell before, now they think I'm an actual devil. I have crapped on the name of the son of god. Kenny heard it, Mr. Thompson heard it, and all of these other morons now know exactly what I think of them. It feels good. It feels freaking fantastic.

And then I see Tess standing about fifteen yards away. She's shaking her head at me. I see tears well up and spill down her face. She gives me a last look, then turns and walks away, shoulders shaking as she goes.

I want to go after her. I want to tell her how sorry I am. How it just came out of my mouth. I said it without thinking.

I don't. I turn and head down the hall, the crowd parting and moving away from me like I've got a contagious disease. I get outside and call my dad. "Come pick me up from school, I need to go home. Now," I say.

Ten minutes later he pulls up in the car. I get in the passenger seat and say, "Drive."

"What happened? Jesus, what happened to your face?"

"I'll tell you when we get home. Just drive."

He looks like he's going to question me again. Instead, he closes his mouth when he sees how close I am to crying.

WHAT TO DO ONCE YOU'VE ACTED LIKE A TOTAL ASS

t's silent on the car ride home. I'm trying not to cry and Dad is trying to give me space. I can feel him looking at me so I turn my head to look out the window.

I'm such a goddamn jerk.

We get home and go inside. I try to go straight upstairs to my bedroom but my dad grabs my arm and pulls me over to the couch.

"Okay. What happened?"

"I don't want to talk about it."

"I just took you out of school in the middle of the day. You look like you're getting a black eye. You're going to talk about it."

I take a deep breath. The last thing I want is to start crying in front of my dad. He gets up, grabs me a glass of water, and sits back down.

"Drink it."

I do. I take a slow breath and feel like I've got control of myself.

"I haven't told you and Mom yet. I've gotten all A's this quarter. I was going to surprise you."

"Ben, that's fantastic," he says smiling.

"Well, until today. A few weeks ago, Mr. Thompson, my science teacher, made me write a paper on why the Bible is important to science. I tried. I really freaking tried. But he wants me to say that the world is only like six thousand years old and that humans didn't evolve and other crazy crap like that. So I wrote a paper on why the facts I know should be enough and how the Bible shouldn't have anything to do with it. He gave me an F. It brings my grade down from an A to a C+."

"That had to make you pretty upset."

"That's not all. As I was leaving the classroom, this kid Kenny, the one I went to church with, who wrote fag on my locker last month, left his backpack in front of the door so that I would trip over it. And now my face and my shoulder are killing me. At that point I kind of lost it and screamed about how much I hate the school and how everyone who believes in god is stupid. Then I got so mad that I yelled Jesus effing Christ in front of like half of the school."

"Oh, Ben."

"Tess heard me and those are pretty much the worst things I could have said."

My dad just looks at me, shaking his head like I'm last week's leftovers and he's deciding whether or not to throw me out. As he gets up to grab me an ice pack from the freezer, he says, "What happened to respecting other people's beliefs?"

"It's not like they're respecting my beliefs!"

"We'll go to the school and talk to your principal about it. Kenny should be punished for bullying you, and it's worrying that he's been getting away with this behavior for so long. However, before we go anywhere, you and I need to talk about a little something called conflict resolution."

I can't stop myself from rolling my eyes. He hands me the ice with a towel over it to put on my cheek.

"Look, at your age and frankly at any age, it can be difficult to manage your emotions. When you get angry you react with anger."

"How else would an angry person react?"

"Acting like a jerk isn't going to make anyone agree with you or want to help you. When you get yelled at, do you listen to what they have to say?"

"I guess not."

"So why should anyone listen to what you have to say? Even if you're right."

I shrug. And now on top of feeling like hell for cursing out god and pretty much the entire school in front of Tess, I now feel like a complete tool for not being able to control myself.

"Next time you feel like that, or if someone confronts you, take a walk. Go tell someone. By yelling at Kenny and offending everyone around you, you became a part of the problem instead of the victim. If it's an issue with your teacher or a student, don't talk to them about it until you've calmed down. Just be the bigger person and walk away. Now, we're going to have some lunch and then go back to the school so we can apologize for your reaction, tell them what Kenny did, and talk about your grade."

"So you agree that I got totally screwed, right? And that Kenny is dangerous."

"Trust me, I'm furious you've got a black eye. That's

absolutely unacceptable. Kenny's parents should be called and he should be suspended. As for the grade, I agree that it seems unfair and like a big drop in your grade from one paper. But we will not be using the word *screwed* when we talk to the principal. Let me make you a sandwich and then I'll call the principal to see if we can meet with him. You just keep that ice on your face."

I eat my sandwich even though I'm starting to feel sick. The entire school probably knows what I said by now and it will get back to the parents. If I wasn't public enemy number one before, I sure am now. Which means that Tess probably wants nothing to do with me anymore.

The whole time we've been dating she's been totally cool with me being an atheist. She lies to her family just to be with me. And here I go and insult her god and her beliefs in the worst way possible. My dad is right. Anger makes me stupid and mean and unworthy of a girl like Tess.

Dad comes in the room and says, "You ready?"

"Do I have a choice?"

"You've always got a choice."

I wonder if all dads say ominous crap like that. It makes you feel like you have a choice. Really, if I chose to stay home, I'd feel even worse.

"Do me a favor and bring the ice. Sympathy points never hurt," he says.

Luckily everyone is in class when we get back to school so I don't have to look anyone in the eye. As we walk into the office, my dad whispers to me, "If I were you, I'd apologize before he asks for one."

The woman at the front desk seems to be expecting us and says, "Principal Willard will see you now."

This is it.

She shows us into the office. We sit down in front of Principal Willard, who puts his hands on the desk and looks at me in that way that grown-ups do.

"I think we all know why we're here," he says.

I suck as much air as I can get into my chest and then spew out a whole bunch of words.

"I'm sorry for saying such horrible things on school grounds this morning. It was mean and disrespectful and I wish I could take it back. There were reasons though. I think you should know the circumstances that led to me saying it."

He leans back in his chair. "Go on," he says.

I tell him about Mr. Thompson and the paper and how his failing me is going to drag down my GPA. How I've made so few friends here because I don't believe in god and how hard it's been being harassed or ignored by practically everyone in the school. I end with how Kenny tripped me outside of Mr. Thompson's class and how everyone watching seemed to think it was some kind of joke.

I lift the ice off my face so he can see how red and messed up it is.

My dad says, "I think you can tell how awful Ben feels about what he said. He was under a lot of emotional stress, though that doesn't excuse his behavior. He knows it's wrong and he's sorry. I hope we can agree that Mr. Thompson's grade was unfair and that Ben shouldn't be penalized for having different views. Also, I think that Kenny should be suspended due to his bullying. Ben's going to have a black eye and his arm is hurting him all because of that boy's prank."

"Ben, do you think a student at your old school

would be given a lesser grade if they said that evolution was wrong on a test?"

"What?"

"If a student took a test at your old school and said that the earth was 6,000 or so years old, do you think they would get that answer incorrect?"

"I'm not sure."

"I am. And the answer is yes. They would get that answer wrong even though they were responding based on what they know to be true. What everyone in this school knows to be true. Now, I've talked to some of your other teachers. You are an impeccable student. However, religion is a part of the curriculum here and I can't just ignore that you don't know it."

"What does that mean?" Dad asks.

"It means that the grade stands. If Ben wants to excel here, he's going to have to learn the material that's presented to him."

"But, sir," says Dad. "Don't you think it's unfair that the hypothetical kid who believed in creation in your scenario got a bad grade? Isn't this just reversed?"

"Ben has enrolled in a religious school. Learn it or leave. That's really all I can tell you."

"I'd like to point out," says Dad, "that you haven't even addressed the fact that my son was physically assaulted at your school."

"I've talked to some witnesses. They say he tripped over a backpack. There is no evidence of anyone touching him so no assault happened."

Dad stands up. "I think Ben would be safer and his work ethic would be more appreciated in a public school. We'd like our tuition for the rest of the semester back."

"You brought your son here so he could learn about values. I'm sorry we couldn't be of more help. However, I'm afraid if you read your agreement you will see that we do not refund. You are paid through December."

"We'll see about that. Come on, Ben. We're leaving."

"I'm not going to the rest of my classes?"

Principal Willard says, "And as for your unfortunate choice of words during your outburst, I'm afraid you're facing a week's suspension. We do not tolerate such language at this institution."

Dad clenches his fist and shakes his head. "So one student injures my son and you do nothing. My son says some hurtful words and he's suspended?"

"As I said, there is no evidence that your son did anything but trip."

"Let's go, Ben. Mr. Willard, thank you for your time."

We walk out and go back to the car. Dad sits still and holds the wheel so tightly that if it were alive he'd have strangled it.

"You thanked him," I say.

"Yes," he says, letting go of the steering wheel and putting on his seat belt.

"Why did you thank him?"

"Because that's what adults do in a bad situation. If I had reacted the way I wanted to, it would have made things worse."

"So being an adult means holding your tongue and letting a guy kick you in the metaphorical balls?"

"Yep. Sometimes that's exactly what it means."

"I think I like my way better."

Chapter 29

DOWN TO ONE

When Mom gets home from work that night, I'm pretty sure that in addition to being pissed at me, she's pissed at Dad. When she left the house this morning I was in school and getting good grades. Now that she's home, I'm suspended and apparently transferring out in December.

We don't even sit down to dinner. There is no dinner. There is just snacking on cereal as I listen to them "discuss" the problem. Me. I'm the problem.

Eventually, after explaining what happened about five times, she calms down. Once she calms down, she finally gets mad at the school instead of at us.

I don't really care at this point. All I want to do is talk to Tess. When I finally escape to my room, she's not online and her curtains are closed. I text her and get no response.

I don't blame her. I wouldn't want to talk to me either.

The crazy thing is that I should be happy. I should be throwing confetti in the air. I'm getting out of this stupid school. I might even go some place where I have more than three friends. Well, one friend now if Tess and Beth are done with me. Which is a real possibility.

James comes home after visiting his mom at the hospital.

"How'd it go?" he asks as he walks into my room.

"I got suspended."

"You've gotta admit. You deserve it."

"For the yelling part. Not for laying into Mr. Thompson. Scumbag. The good news is that my parents are on my side." I pause for a second, not knowing how he's going to take this next part. "They're sending me to public school in January."

It's silent for a few seconds before James says, "That's what you wanted."

"Yeah," I say, trying not to sound too excited. He'll be on his own again. "You'll still be at my house all the time though, right?"

"Yeah. 'Course."

I check my phone for the tenth time in the last hour.

"Nothing yet from Tess."

"That's probably going to take some time and a lot of groveling," he says.

"Did you talk to her?"

"No. But I saw her and her face was all red and Beth was leading her outside. They both ignored me."

James says the words with anger in his voice. Damn it. Beth.

"I'm sorry about Saturday, man. I guess it's off."

James doesn't disagree with me. He just says, "I've got to go do some homework."

I totally ruined his chances of even having a conversation with Beth. I mean, I know I messed up my relationship, but James was so into finally getting a chance to hang out with her. It's my fault he won't get to. I screwed up everything.

I pull out my phone again. No texts.

Perfect. Looks like I'm on my own again.

The next day after school James comes home and gives me my homework.

"So what's the word at school?" I ask.

"That you're a compete tool. You're like the most hated kid in town."

"Have you talked to Tess?"

He breathes deep, takes an envelope out of his bag, and hands it to me.

"Sorry man."

"She broke up with me, didn't she?"

"Read the letter."

"Just tell me."

"Yeah. She broke up with you."

I sit down on my bed and put my hands on my head. "I deserve it."

"Yeah. You going to read the letter?"

"Not now."

"Do you want to watch a movie or something?"

James always knows when to push and when to lay off.

"Yeah, sure," I say glumly.

"Okay. You pick."

Suddenly the doorbell rings. My heart jumps and I think for a second that it could be Tess. Maybe she wants to talk. To give me a chance to explain.

I run down the stairs, taking them three or four at a

time and almost knock my mom down on the way to the door. "I've got it," I say.

I open the door ready to say how sorry I am, but it's not her. It's Trent.

"Hey. Can you come outside for a minute?" he says.

"Uh. Sure. Yeah."

I grab my coat, put on my shoes, and meet Trent on the front steps.

"I wanted to tell you in person outside of school that I'm sorry, but you're out of the talent show."

"What?" I say, immediately feeling my blood get hot and my face go red. "I've worked my ass off for that show. These kids are going to love my act."

"We want parents to come and give us money, and what you did, that messes with the entire show. Everyone in town knows about what happened. I can't let it ruin our chance to raise some money for these kids. That's what this show is all about."

"Look, I know I messed up and I feel horrible for saying what I said. Tess won't even talk to me. I can't fix it if I'm blacklisted. I mean, I already got suspended. That should be enough."

Trent looks genuinely upset as he listens to me. Not like he hates me, but like he hates that he's kicking me out.

"I'm sorry, man. It's not going to happen. It's not my decision."

"It's your show."

"I wish. Frank said you're out."

"Yeah. Okay. Thanks for telling me. And for coming over to do it in person."

"Sure thing." He looks like he's about to say something else but shakes his head and just says, "Later."

I sit down on the front step and try not to scream. Screaming is what got me into this freaking mess. So instead I think. I plan. I plot. There has to be a way to fix this.

Chapter 30

BACK TO THE SOBER LIFE

I t turns out that the kids were right about me going to hell. When I come back from suspension, school is pretty much what I imagine hell to be. I just didn't have to die to get here.

Not only am I out of the talent show, the only thing I had to keep me going, but now the entire school is against me. Not like before when they just didn't care about me. Now I get dirty looks and insults as I walk down the hall. "Loser." "No one wants you here." "All fags go to hell." Stuff like that. Not that I even care about any of them. The only person I really care about is Tess.

Tess has blocked me online, won't answer my texts, and keeps her curtains closed. She'd rather be vitamin D deficient than risk looking at my face.

The only good thing is that I'll be out of here in a month. I'll be switching to a public school. I'm pretty sure most of those students will still be religious. At least it won't mess up my grades. And I'll still have James to hang out with after school.

Also, I had a ton of time to study the McBride DVD and practice my moves. Frank booted me out of the talent show, but I'll be damned if that's going to stop me. This school has done nothing but kick me. Before I leave I want to do that talent show and prove to everyone that I'm not a heartless sinner. I just have to find a way. There's still one illusion that I just can't get. My hands aren't moving fast enough and James can see what I'm doing every time. I need Margaret's help to figure that one out. This show is going to be my finale. My good-bye to this place.

Soon I'll have no more religion being shoved in my face at school. No more prayers or Bible stuff. In fact, it's against the law to pray in school. I never understood that law before. Now I think it's a way of preventing kids from feeling left out. If you're the only Jewish second-grader in school and everyone is praying to Jesus all the time it could get pretty lonely.

For now I am that lonely. James continues to be awesome. He's also kind of mad that I'm leaving. Tess hasn't stopped talking to him, but to everyone else he's seen as a crazy person for hanging out with me. Plus, his mom gets out of rehab today, just in time for Thanksgiving this weekend. He hasn't said much about it, but I can tell he's nervous.

I'm heading East tomorrow to visit my sister at Sarah Lawrence and then we're going up to Boston to do Thanksgiving at my aunt and uncle's house. Which means that James is going to have to deal with his mom by himself.

After school, which can't end fast enough with Tess avoiding eye contact with me every time we pass each other in the hall, my mom picks us up and we go to the hospital to pick up James's mom. She's sitting in the lobby looking at her feet. She doesn't even notice us as we walk up to her. James puts his hand on her shoulder and says, "Hey, Mom."

She looks up and smiles at him. Her eyes are watery and she makes no move to stand up.

"Are you ready to go?" he asks.

She looks over at my mom and me briefly. My mom takes the hint and pulls me a few steps away to give them some privacy.

She looks terrified. James gives her a hug, takes her bag, and holds her hand to walk her out to the car. I sit in the front seat with my mom and James takes the back with his mom, who looks out the window like she hasn't really seen this town in years. Like it's all new to her.

"Your son was a perfect guest," Mom says to Mrs. Bullard.

"Thank you so much for having him," says Mrs. Bullard, softly. "Really, your kindness won't be forgotten. Heaven holds a place for people like you."

My mom smiles and says, "He's been a wonderful friend to Ben."

The rest of the drive is silent and kind of awkward. We finally get to James's house and pull up in front.

James looks at me like he might just barf on his front lawn. I give him an encouraging smile.

"James," says my mom. "I picked up some groceries for you both since you haven't been home in a while. They're in the trunk. Can you be a dear and grab them?"

Mrs. Bullard can't quite manage to make eye contact

with my mom but she does reach up to the front seat to squeeze her shoulder.

"You're too kind," she says.

"Nonsense. Happy to help."

Mrs. Bullard gets out of the car and slowly walks up to the house. James closes the trunk and gives me a nod as he jogs up to his mom to walk with her. He puts the groceries down, opens the door, and Mrs. Bullard steps in.

"You think she'll be okay?"

"I hope so, for both their sakes. You just keep a close eye on him, okay?"

"Okay."

Chapter 31

COLLEGE KIDS ARE SMARTER THAN ME

The next morning I get on a plane to New York. In fact, I get to go on a plane by myself to visit Emily. My parents are meeting us in a few days once we get to Boston. Should be interesting since Emily still hasn't bothered mentioning to our parents that she's got a girlfriend. It has to come up sooner or later.

Emily doesn't meet me at the airport. She does meet me at the train station in Bronxville, once I've taken a bus, a subway, and then a train. Not overwhelming at all for my first time in New York City.

She's standing on the platform with another girl. A really, really good-looking girl. Long brown hair, a short skirt with thick striped stockings, and a tight sweater. I pull my shoulders back and hold onto my bag, as if it isn't so heavy that it's been killing my arm since the airport. Which it has.

Emily hasn't seen me yet and just as I get within ten feet of them, she leans in and plants a fat kiss on the hot girl's lips. Freaking great.

I drop my bag on the ground and sit on the bench

behind me. Em finishes kissing the hot girl and looks around. Perhaps she's finally noticed that most of the people have stepped off the platform and she hasn't seen her little brother yet. Not that she was trying hard to find me.

She turns. "You don't have a hug for your sister?"

"You were busy."

"Oh, whatever. Come here!"

She pulls me in for a big hug but right now I just feel awkward. She was just kissing a hotter girl than I have ever even talked to. It's probably against some law to get tingly at the thought of your sister's girlfriend. And then to have your sister hug you while you're tingly? That's just gross.

Em lets me go and pushes me toward the girl.

"This is Jamie. Jamie, this is my brother Ben."

"Nice to meet you. Sorry for accosting your sis right when you arrived."

"From my view, it looked like it was her fault."

"It usually is." They smile at each other.

Gross.

Jamie sees my reaction, and says, "Sorry. No little brother wants to see his sister with anyone."

"Ha. Yeah," I say, awkwardly. "I'm glad she met someone though."

"I kind of want to send a thank you letter to the housing people for putting us together," she jokes, smiling at Emily again.

It's already nine o'clock so by the time we get back to campus and eat some food at the pub, it's almost time to go to sleep. It's my first night on a college campus and I'm too tired to do anything. How lame.

My sister lays out the blow-up mattress while Jamie

changes in the bathroom. I stand in a corner of the room wondering how I'm going to sleep at all with my sister and her girlfriend snuggling three feet away from me. Her ridiculously hot girlfriend who has just come out of the bathroom in a tank top and tiny shorts. I look away toward the wall but it's covered with a bunch of pictures of hot girls out of Vogue or something.

Plus, the name of the dorm she lives in is Titsworth. For real. Titsworth.

"Do I really have to sleep here?" I ask.

"What's the problem?"

"It's just. This is your room and you share it with your girlfriend."

"So?"

"I'd just rather not sleep while you two make out."

"You think we want to make out with my little brother in the room? We're going to go to sleep. That's all."

"Please."

"It's this or Ed's room. Just so you know, he's gay too."

"Does Ed have a boyfriend?"

"Not right now."

"Then yeah, I'd like to sleep in Ed's room."

She rolls her eyes and picks up the phone. Five minutes later I'm down the hall pumping air into my mattress in Ed's room. He's reading. At least he doesn't have any half-naked pictures of men on his walls. He's got more class than my sister.

Ed looks up. "I have a PlayStation if you're interested. Unless you're tired."

I am tired but I'm also feeling too excited about being out of Forest Ridge to want to go to sleep right away.

"Thanks. You want to play?"

"Let me just finish this chapter."

I set up the controller and pick a game. Ed is no newbie. He must have two dozen games lined up under his bed. I put one in and fiddle with the controllers to get used to it. My dad would rather I study than play games and no matter how many, *But Dad, it helps with hand-eye coordination* arguments I make, he still says no. Which means, I'll probably suck.

Ed puts his book down on the desk and turns to me.

"So why are you sleeping here tonight instead of in your sister's room?"

Ed apparently likes to get straight to the point.

"It was just kind of weird."

He nods like he knows what I mean.

"Jamie is hot," he says.

I shrug, not wanting to agree so blatantly.

"Emily said that your parents moved to Forest Ridge. How's that going for you?"

"It could be better."

Ed opens up his mini-fridge to take out a soda. There's a six-pack of beer inside too.

"Can I have one?" I ask.

"Sure," he says, handing me a soda.

"I meant a beer."

"You twenty-one?"

"No. I'm visiting college. Isn't this what I'm supposed to be doing?"

"If you think college is about drinking beer, then all you're going to get out of it is being drunk."

"You drink."

"I'm twenty-one. All you high schoolers think that drinking is about getting drunk. When you get older, drunk is kind of dumb."

"I saw a whole group of drunk Sarah Lawrence kids earlier tonight."

"They're dumb."

I think of James's mom and of James getting drunk while we were cleaning and feel kind of guilty for even asking.

Ed starts playing the game, a first-person shooter. He kills me in the first twenty seconds.

"The only thing I know about Colorado Springs is that it's home to a ton of right-wing Christians," says Ed. "Have you accepted Jesus Christ as your personal savior yet?" he says sarcastically.

"I'm an atheist."

"Not even agnostic. A full-blown atheist?"

"What's the difference?"

"An atheist believes there is definitely no god. An agnostic throws his hands up in the air and says, 'Hell if I know.'"

"Well, I guess I don't know. No one does. That's my problem."

"Your problem with what?"

"Religion. There are so many and they all believe they're right. They can't all be right. I may not believe in a god but if I'm wrong so is most of the population who chose wrong."

"Not that much diversity in terms of religious choices in Forest Ridge," says Ed.

"I have one atheist friend and that's about it."

"Who do the kids make fun of more?"

"Definitely me. I'm the most hated kid in school. Though he's mostly ignored by everyone, so also not a good situation." I take a drink of my soda. "What religion are you?" I ask.

"My Dad's Jewish and my mom is some sort of new-age crystal worshipper. Don't ask. And I just don't care."

"So an atheist?"

"If you had to put a label on it."

"Do people hate you for it?"

"No. But plenty hate me for being gay. And most of the people who care about that are religious."

"Why do you think they care?"

"Because they believe every word from a book written a few thousand years ago that says being gay is a sin."

"Don't you just hate religion?"

"Religion isn't the problem. Plenty of people are religious and totally cool with gay people. For the most part I've found that those who are against gay people aren't cool with anyone different from them, and they use old books to defend their hate. That way they can pretend it isn't hate speech, they're just protecting American values or some crap that they can twist around for their own purpose."

"Doesn't that make you mad?"

"'Course it does. But things are changing fast. Soon, people like me will be able to get married in every single state."

"Things aren't changing fast in Forest Ridge. I'm hated for not believing in god, I can't even imagine what they'd do to a gay kid."

"There is always going to be someone who has a problem with who you are or what you believe. But you'll go to college, meet people you relate to, and life gets better. It really does."

"Can you tell Emily that? She hasn't come out yet to our parents."

"She will."

"Can you tell her that it's going to be fine?"

"I don't care how cool your parents are. Every kid is a little scared of coming out. She told you first. That must mean she really trusts you."

I pick up the controller and we start playing another game. I look over at Ed, "So did you know you were gay in high school?"

"Yes. But I went to school in New York City at a performing arts high school. I wasn't out of the norm."

"I wish I could go to one of those."

"Everyone is strange to someone. A right-wing Christian would have been torn apart at my school. Being a minority sucks. Hell, your sister gets made fun of here for being vegan. Here!"

"I make fun of her for being vegan."

"Do you know why she's vegan?"

"She likes animals."

Ed stands up, grabs his computer, and searches for a video.

"Watch this."

The video shows a warehouse full of chickens. Some dead. Some look half dead. Chickens in cages by the thousand. They sit in their own crap, and in some cases in the same cage as a dead chicken. And so they don't attack each other while being piled into small cages, half of their beaks are cut off.

All the chickens do is lay eggs. If they don't lay eggs they are starved until their body is shocked into laying more. Those are the females. The males are killed as soon as they're hatched, thrown in the garbage, and crushed under their own weight. I press stop.

"Wow."

"Yeah," says Ed.

"I don't think I wanted to see that."

"Yeah, that's how I felt. Now you know, you can't un-see it."

"I sort of wish I could."

"Want to see another one about pig farms?" asks Ed. He searches for another video.

"I guess. Just do me a favor and don't tell my sister we watched these."

He laughs. "Sure thing."

Chapter 32

PEOPLE DON'T ASK TO BE HATED

The next morning Ed and I meet Em and Jamie at the pub for breakfast. At first I want to order a breakfast sandwich. Then I think about those stupid videos from last night. The idea of eating a pig right now makes me want to puke. Even though I'm drooling at the smell of bacon, I order a bagel with peanut butter.

It's Tuesday morning and the campus is already emptying out. Today is the last day of classes before everyone is off for the holiday.

Em and Jamie kiss good-bye and Ed gives me a fist bump. I've never actually met anyone before who gives fist bumps but it makes me feel momentarily cooler.

We head to Em's poetry class, her one and only class of the day. Each student reads his or her work out loud and then they all talk about it and give feedback. Some of them make no sense to me. Others make a lot of sense. One guy writes about his man parts. Seriously. A whole poem about what he's got and what he does with it. I didn't know you could write poems about that kind of stuff.

My sister tells the guy that he should use the clinical word for male genitalia instead of slang. That it would work better in the poem. He nods and writes it down.

My sister just told a guy what he should be calling his wang. I had to stop myself from laughing.

After class as we walk down to the other end of campus my sister asks, "So what did you think?"

"It was weird."

"Why was it weird?"

"I just didn't know people wrote poems like that."

"How many poems have you actually read?"

"Just a few I've read for school."

"Well, pick up some Ginsberg or some Sharon Olds. You'll see that poems aren't just like the boring ones you read in school. They can be whatever you want. As long as the language is great the subject will be meaningful. Truth will be found."

"Truth?"

"Poems are about emotional truth. At least to me. Getting to the substance and sharing your vision of the world."

"I wanted to laugh at that guy's poem. He talked about his . . ."

"It made you uncomfortable."

"People don't usually talk about that."

"Great art is about saying the difficult thing. About not being afraid."

We walk down to the art building so she can show me around the printmaking studio.

I keep thinking about truth. About thinking the difficult thing and saying it out loud. That takes guts. And a little bit of insanity. How many people actually tell the truth in their daily lives? Tess sure doesn't. Neither does James. I avoid the truth unless someone like Tess's dad or Mr. Thompson asks me directly. We don't lie, not exactly. We just steer clear of saying anything at all. Not even Emily tells the truth. She hasn't told our parents that she's gay.

We get to the studio and she leads me inside. Emily has been doing woodcuts and something called intaglio where you take a metal plate, mark it with acid, ink it up, and then run it under a press. The image you make with the acid shows up on the paper. It's pretty freaking awesome.

"I spend about twelve hours a week in here," she says as she inks up one of her metal plates.

"That's a lot of time."

"Yep. I love it. How is your magic coming along? You still practicing a lot?"

"I'm performing at a fundraiser in two and a half weeks actually."

"That's great. Your first real performance."

"Well, technically I was booted from the talent show. I'm trying to get back in. It might not even change anything. Everyone there hates me, including Tess."

"I'm sure that's not true."

"You know what I did."

"You said a swear word. Big deal."

"I didn't just curse. I told a bunch of people that everything they believed is stupid and wrong. How would you feel if someone yelled some homophobic slurs and threw the F word in there just to drive the point home?"

"I'd be mad."

"That's what it's like for them. It's that bad."

"So Tess is still not talking to you?"

"Definitely not."

"Have you tried talking to her?"

"I've texted her, I've left notes in her locker, I've sent messages through James, and I've emailed her like three apologies. Nothing."

"Man, she must really be mad."

"Well, I'll be in public school starting January fifth, so she won't have to see me for much longer. She can go back to lying to her family so she doesn't rock the boat."

"It can't be easy for her," says Em as she places the plate onto the press and puts a piece of dampened paper over it. She cranks it through the press. "You said her brother is an atheist?"

"Yep, that's why she hasn't seen him in years. Her family disowned him. They don't want him to be a bad influence on the rest of the kids. We were planning on going to his wedding in a few weeks. Pete's going to be home then, and he said he'd take us."

"Her parents aren't going?" asks Em. "To their own son's wedding?"

"They won't have anything to do with him."

"It would be like Mom and Dad disowning me because I'm gay. Well, except I didn't choose to be gay."

"I didn't choose to be an atheist. People don't usually choose to be the thing that's going to make their life harder."

"Being gay isn't hard," she says.

"Then why haven't you told Mom and Dad yet?"

She ignores the question and pulls the paper off the plate.

"Exactly," I say. "In some ways it's harder, right? You have to deal with stupid people. Maybe not at

Sarah Lawrence, but out in the world you will. You're terrified Mom and Dad are going to freak out."

"Wouldn't you be?"

"Why don't you tell them this weekend?"

"We'll be at Aunt Lisa's house."

"So?"

"So just because I'm willing to come out to my parents doesn't mean I'm ready to come out to the whole family."

"When has anyone in our family ever said a mean thing about gay people?"

"They don't know any!"

"They're for gay marriage."

"That doesn't mean they want their daughter to be gay."

"You're not giving them enough credit."

"Maybe, but it's my choice so drop it."

She grabs the metal plate and washes off the leftover ink.

"Can I see what you made?" I ask.

She points to the table. "Over there."

"What is this?"

"It's a map of Massachusetts according to me."

The outline is of Massachusetts for sure. The inside has all sorts of different designs. Boston is a sort of crisscross pattern while right outside of Boston, where we lived, is less jagged looking. Softer. Each area feels different based on the etchings she did on the metal.

"It's really freaking cool," I say. "Can I have this?"

"Yeah. There's a bit too much ink so I have to make another anyway."

I stare at the paper, still a little wet in my hand. "Do you miss home?" I ask her.

"A lot."

"Me too."

"I've got to make a few more prints. After we'll get some food and head back to the dorm. Watch a movie or something, okay? It's just you and me tonight."

"So we're meeting Mom and Dad tomorrow night?"

"Yep, at Aunt Lisa's."

"Any chance we could go to Boston a bit early tomorrow?"

"Sure. You have big plans?"

"I just really need to see Seth and Margaret."

Chapter 33

HOW TO TELL AN OLD FRIEND THAT HE'S STUPID

The next morning Em and I get up super early, get in the car, and head up past Boston to our hometown. As we get closer, I get more and more nervous and start to sweat. I want to see Margaret. I want her to show me what I'm doing wrong with the harder card moves. First, I need Seth to stop being a jealous jerk. Not to mention that I'd really like to have my friends back.

Just being in New England feels good. No Tess across the street ignoring me. No signs that say "Jesus Loves You" along the highway. I feel like I'm home. The trees are different here. The buildings are older. In Colorado it's like everything was built in the last fifty years. Boston has buildings that are old America. Churches actually look like churches. Not huge boxes that look like Walmart.

We drive through town and Emily drops me off in front of my old school. I would be here right now if we hadn't moved to Colorado.

It's nearly 11:30. Lunch is starting in a few minutes. I hope Margaret and Seth still eat lunch on the lower level behind the gym. I walk in and sit on the floor just around the corner so I'll be able to see them come in.

Ten minutes go by. I don't really want to go up to the cafeteria and do the whole catch up thing with everyone I used to know. What would I say? *I'm a total outcast at my new school. Thanks for asking.*

I'm just about to head in when the door opens. Seth and Margaret are holding hands and laughing as they step inside and kiss each other.

They haven't seen me yet and I don't call out. All I can think of is how this is what Tess and I were never able to have. A normal relationship. Maybe it's good that we broke up. And here Seth and Margaret are, kissing and hanging out in public like it's the most normal thing in the world. They don't know how lucky they are. I really miss Tess.

Finally Seth notices me. His smile turns into a *what the hell are you doing here* face mixed with a *I know I'm a jerk for ignoring you but I won't admit it* face.

"You don't call? You don't text?" I ask with a pissed-off smirk.

He just stares at me.

"Hey, Margaret," I say more calmly.

"Hey, Ben."

"Do you mind giving us a few minutes?"

"No problem."

She kisses Seth on the cheek, whispers something in his ear, and heads inside.

We stand there for a few seconds silently. I have no idea what to do. You can't just say, *Don't be jealous of my sexy self. I'm sure your girlfriend isn't hot for me anymore.* But you can't ignore it either.

So I say an equally unlikely thing.

"My girlfriend dumped me a few weeks ago."

He looks at me for a second, like he's deciding whether or not to play along.

"What desperate girl would go out with you?"

"A cute, nice, smart girl. Now, nobody."

"That sucks."

"I'm hungry. My sister and I just drove up from New York. Any chance you'd split your sandwich?"

He sits down in our old spot and hands me half of his food.

"Your mom and my dad love the pb and j."

"It's the lazy parent's lunch," he says.

"Ha. Yeah."

We both take a bite and sit silently while we eat.

"So, anything new here?" I ask.

He takes another bite of his sandwich and chews slowly before answering.

"Margaret and I are dating."

"I sorta got that from the kissing. I always thought you two would be good together. Is she making you do your homework?"

"Yes! She comes over with her backpack and makes sure we're both done with our homework before she'll even kiss me."

"That's a good motivator."

"I've never gotten my homework done so fast in my life."

We both eat silently for a minute.

"How's your new school?" Seth asks carefully.

"Everyone there hates me."

"Why?"

"Because I don't believe in god. And because I yelled

some pretty awful stuff in front of a bunch of people that was totally offensive."

"Why'd you do that?"

"A lot of reasons. My science teacher failed me for not writing that dinosaurs and humans lived on earth at the same time, and this ass at school tripped me with his bag so I fell on my face."

"Damn. Do you have any friends?"

Seth looks a little guilty as he asks. Like he's now realizing what a tool he's been for ignoring me these last few months.

"One. He's awesome."

"One isn't bad."

I tell him about James and about Tess and what happened. About how I'll be starting public school in January. After a few minutes, it's like I never left. Like he never ignored me. A part of me wants to punch him in the face for cutting me out of his life the way he did. Another part of me is just happy to have my friend back.

"So before I leave for public school I'm doing a magic show in my school's talent show. At least, I'm trying to figure out a way for them to let me back in so I can perform in it."

"Why don't you bail? I mean, if none of them want you there."

"It's not fair for them to kick me out. I've been punished already and I worked my butt off for that magic show."

"It will be your first real show."

"I know and I've been practicing a lot. I just need help on one part."

"Yeah?"

"From the best magician we know. "

"Oh."

"I was hoping I could tag along with you guys tonight and Margaret could show me what I'm doing wrong."

"Yeah, I guess. We were just going to hang out in my basement tonight and watch a movie."

"So it's cool?"

"Yeah. It's cool."

"Great."

"I should get to class."

"I'll see you tonight then. Seven?"

"Sounds good."

Chapter 34

LIKE IT WAS BEFORE. SORT OF.

That night Margaret, Seth, and I hang out for hours. We watch some slasher movie and then end up talking the way we did before I moved. Before everything changed. I'm feeling so nostalgic for my life before I moved, but then during the movie Margaret leans on Seth's shoulder, and he puts his arm around her.

All I can think about is Tess. We've never watched a movie together, and now we probably never will. I thought being on the other side of the country would make things easier. Instead I just miss her more.

I reach inside my bag and hold the letter she wrote me. It's still sealed. I haven't had the guts to open it.

I know she broke up with me, but the idea of reading how badly I hurt her is just too much to handle. So I've been keeping it in the side pocket of my bag along with my magic stuff. All the things that are important to me.

After the movie, Seth goes upstairs to grab us some snacks. Margaret and I start on the trick that I need to master if I'm not going to make a total fool of myself during the show. She does it perfectly and makes it look really easy. I botch it like thirty times in a row before it finally starts coming together.

"It took me a lot of practice before I got good at this one," says Margaret, probably to make me feel better.

Seth brings down some chicken fingers. They smell really good. I'm hungry and kind of drooling in my mouth from the smell. I think I liked life better before I saw those videos. I mean, once you know something you can't unknow it. What kind of a person finds out about something terrible and then does the terrible thing anyway?

"Not hungry?" asks Seth.

"Got anything else?" I ask.

"Maybe. Go upstairs and look."

Ugh. Emily is going to love this in her annoying *I was right, you were wrong* kind of way.

I head up to the kitchen and raid the pantry like I used to do three times a week back when I lived here and grab some chips. Salty. Fatty. And they will make me stop drooling for chicken.

By about midnight I'm halfway through the bag of chips and my moves are finally passable. They're not perfect, but with Margaret's help placing my fingers and angling my hands toward my audience of one, for the first time I feel like I'm not going to make a fool out of myself. It's been so long that Seth and Margaret just start clapping. Mostly because Margaret needs to get home and Seth wants to go to sleep. I'm wired and feel so excited that I finally have a handle on what could be my finale for the show so I just keep practicing until my fingers are tired.

Margaret heads home and Seth goes up to sleep. I

stay down in the basement practicing the whole routine for another hour and then crash on the couch.

That's the best part of old friends. You can sleep at their house without even really asking. Even when fourteen hours earlier you weren't talking to them. Or rather, they weren't talking to you.

As good as it feels to be here, I wonder how James is doing.

I look at my watch. 1:30 a.m. It's earlier in Colorado so I give him a call.

"Hello?" says a very sleepy voice.

"Hey, man. It's me. Sorry I woke you up."

"It's okay. Is something wrong?"

"No. I'm at Seth's and just wanted to see how you're doing."

"Okay so far. I'm trying to keep her busy. I took her to church today. Which sucks for me but is good for her."

"Good. I'm glad," I say. "How is Holly doing?"

"Your mom dropped her off earlier tonight. She keeps looking out the window for you guys. I think she's starting to relax. How is it going with Seth and Margaret? Good I guess if he's letting you sleep over."

"Yeah. And Margaret helped me with that trick so I won't look stupid in front of the whole school."

"Now you're worried about looking stupid in front of the whole school? Where was that thought a few weeks ago?"

"See, I called you up to be all nice and you say a thing like that."

"It's true!"

"So true it kills me."

"And what makes you think anyone is going to let you onstage?"

"I'm still working on that part."

"Work faster."

"I'm the master of the last-minute plan. At least I hope I am. Right now, I've got nothing."

"Have you opened the letter yet?"

"No."

"Grow a pair and get it done. Rip the Band-Aid off fast."

"Is Tess still going to her brother's wedding?"

"I don't know."

"She should."

"She was counting on you."

"Trust me. I know it. Anyway, I just called to make sure things were cool at your house."

"Thanks, man."

I hang up and take Tess's letter out of my bag. I come *this close* to opening it. Then I change my mind. It's time to get some sleep. Tomorrow is Thanksgiving.

Chapter 35

PARENTS ARE PEOPLE TOO

In the morning Emily picks me up and we go get Mom and Dad from the airport just before lunch. They left Colorado at like four o'clock this morning. They could have gotten here yesterday but I think my mom wanted to avoid cooking. My aunt likes to put all the women in the kitchen while the guys sit on the couch and watch football. It makes my mom crazy. Especially since she's not into cooking and my aunt always points out everything she does wrong. So this year she just skipped that part.

On the way to my aunt's, Emily stops at a vegan restaurant to pick something up for lunch. My aunt always makes enough food for twenty people, but none of it ever seems to be animal-free for my sister. Either the vegetables are cooked with chicken stock or something has lard in it. My aunt hasn't changed my grandma's recipes.

I go in with her and say kind of casually, "That looks pretty good. Order me one too?"

"Seriously?" she asks.

"Just be happy I'm not eating meat today."

"Touché. You're right. A second seitan picatta coming right up."

She looks at me a little strangely, so I pretend to study the menu until the food is ready. Then it's back out to the car.

"Ben got something too," says Em.

"Your aunt's not going to like that," says Mom, kind of smiling.

"You're terrible," says Dad.

"Who me?" says Mom. She grins and turns to me. "Have you spoken to James?"

"Yeah. They're doing good, I think."

"Glad to hear that," she says. "You know, I actually miss having him in the house."

"Pete will be home next week," says Em. "You'll have more kids in the house soon."

"He's hardly a kid," says Mom.

"Oh come on. Even forty-year-olds are kids in their parents' house. I'm jealous. I won't get to see him until Christmas."

The car is quiet for a moment before Dad starts in with the questions.

"So Emily, we haven't heard much from you this semester. Classes keeping you busy?"

"Yeah," says Mom. "We sent you to Sarah Lawrence and you disappeared!"

"Yep, it's a lot of classwork," says Emily. "It's been crazy."

"Glad you're getting the most out of it," says Mom. "We just miss you."

"Her friends are really nice," I say. "Her roommate and their friend Ed."

"You haven't told us much about your roommate," Mom says. Emily gives me a nasty look. I smile and shrug.

"She's great," Em says. "Everyone is great. My teachers. The students. I couldn't ask for a better school. Plus, I've done a good job of not getting suspended."

Emily looks at me and grins back, very happy with herself.

"Public school will be a better fit for Ben," says Dad. "This private school just didn't allow for people to be different like your old school did. That was our mistake."

"Thanks, Dad," I say. "You've always been really good at being nice to people who are different."

"Um. Thanks, Ben. We try."

Emily rolls her eyes but instead of mocking her some more I look at her and nod encouragingly.

She shakes her head. *Come on*, I mouth silently. *Before we get there.* Her face turns red. She opens her mouth to speak. Nothing comes out.

I nod again and then say, "Go on."

"Go on what?" says Dad.

Em gives me a death stare.

"Ben wants me to tell you that I've been dating someone," she says, her face now red and blotchy. "It's new so I didn't want to say anything."

"That's great!" says Mom. "What's he like?"

Emily looks like she's going to spill and tell them about Jamie. Then she totally backs down.

"Great. Really wonderful. Does photography. Is a great writer."

"Where is he from?"

"Oregon."

"What's his name?" asks Dad.

"Uh. Jamie."

I'm just shaking my head at Em, like *really?* She gives me a look that says *back the hell off*, so I do. I don't say another word. Not a single pronoun. Now she won't look at me. She's all quiet and mad and my parents just keep asking her questions, until they get the feeling she doesn't want to talk about it anymore. Which makes the car ride awkward, cause before there was almost nothing my sister wouldn't talk to my parents about.

Finally we get to my aunt's house and we can all get out of the car and pretend that nothing weird just happened.

My aunt doesn't even let us get inside before she's hugging us and taking our coats and bags. She's just as annoyed as Mom thought she'd be that my sister brought food, and when she finds out I did too her face goes tight. It doesn't even matter that without the food we brought there wouldn't be a single thing that Emily could eat.

My aunt drags Mom straight into the kitchen, even when Dad offers to help instead. "It's not like this is 1950. Men can help in the kitchen, Sis." She just waves him off and pulls Mom away.

My uncle, Dad, Em, and me sit in the living room while the Macy's Day parade plays on TV. Uncle Matt and Dad talk about Pete and politics and other stuff. Emily just sits in the corner looking pissed off.

Uncle Matt tells Dad that he got a new computer and can't get it synched up with his printer, so Dad goes upstairs with him to try and get it to work.

When they are out of range I say, "You should have told them."

"Screw you, Ben. Seriously, in a car? You want me to tell them in a freaking car? It's bigger news than that. You want Dad to drive off the road?"

"He wouldn't."

"It's my news, okay? It's my life. Not yours. So just shut it. Don't say another word. I have to tell them now, but I'll do it when I want to. Not when you want me to. That was messed up."

"I was just trying to help."

"Unless you bring home your boyfriend, don't pretend like you know what this is like. It's scary to tell them. Even though 99% of me thinks they will be fine with it, that other 1% is scared that they won't look at me the same. That they'll judge me."

"Okay. I won't say anything. No more pressure."

It's silent for a few minutes. Emily still isn't looking at me and I feel like crap for trying to force her. The parade plays and both of us look at the TV without really watching.

Finally, like a peace offering, Emily asks, "So, no meat for you today?"

"Nope."

"Why not?"

"Someone just told me that meat is made of animals."

She laughs. "You just realized that?"

"I'm not saying I'm a vegetarian or anything."

"'Course not."

"I'm just not eating meat today."

"That's a good start."

Chapter 36

LETTERS ARE MEANT TO BE OPENED

The rest of the day goes pretty decently. There are no more awkward questions for Emily, and besides a few dirty looks from my aunt for ignoring her turkey and ham, the evening goes off without a hitch. The seitan thing Em got for me ends up tasting a lot like chicken, which is fine by me.

My aunt sets up the guest rooms for us so we can crash. I think we all liked it better when we could go home at the end of a family holiday. Especially, Mom. My aunt is already talking about what they'll make for breakfast in the morning so Mom says, "Actually, we were going to take the kids out for breakfast to celebrate their good grades this semester."

My aunt looks annoyed, but that's the usual face she makes.

Once all the cleaning is done (not that I helped or anything), I go upstairs and find Em reading on the other bed in the room we're sharing.

She puts her book down.

"I don't like lying to them," she says. "I can't imagine telling them either."

"I know you can do it."

"I don't want to do it. I don't want to have to say, *Hey, Mom and Dad, I'm into girls in the gay way.* That's just so not . . . not . . ."

Em looks totally frozen. Her eyes are wide and she's staring at the door. I look behind me and see Dad. His face looks like someone just told him he has cancer. Like he had a stroke. Not like he's angry or upset. Like he's too shocked to even be able to understand what was just said.

Em says, "Dad, I, I . . ."

"Dad, say something," I say. "Anything." Before Emily starts crying, I think.

"Are you okay? I was going to tell you. I just didn't want to do it over the phone, and then the car wasn't the right place either. I was going to tell you."

"You think you're gay?" he says finally, putting his hand through his hair.

"I don't think," says Em, kind of defensively. "I am gay."

"You weren't gay when you went away to school."

"Yes. I was," says Em, looking more and more angry.

It's silent for a minute while Dad just stands there looking stupid and Em just sits there looking furious and hurt and like she's going to cry any second.

Then Mom comes in, and not even noticing that anything weird is happening, she says, "Your aunt wants to know if you all have toothbrushes, because if anyone forgot them she has some extras in the cupboard below the sink." She finally looks around at each of us and says, "What's wrong?"

No one says anything. Em doesn't make a sound. Her eyes are red and she won't make eye contact with anyone.

Mom looks at Dad. "What's wrong? What happened? Is Pete okay?"

"Pete's fine," says Em. "Dad's mad at me."

"I'm not mad at you," he finally says, his voice kind of foggy.

"Right," says Em. "See Mom, Dad just overheard me talking to Ben about the fact that I'm gay and how I was too scared to tell you because I was worried about what you might think. Glad to know I wasn't scared for nothing."

Mom looks surprised but rebounds fast. She says, "Of course you shouldn't be scared. We love you." She goes over to the bed, sits next to Em, and puts her arm around her. Emily starts crying, fully crying.

"It's okay," says Mom. "It's okay."

"Dad doesn't think so. Look at him."

Mom looks at Dad, who still has an expression on his face that says he is not happy. In fact he looks kind of sad.

"Excuse us a moment," says Mom as she pulls him out of the room.

I sit still while Em cries. I don't even know what to say.

"I told you," she says. "He's horrified."

"He didn't look horrified. I don't know what he looked like. Mom was fine. That's something."

"What about Dad? What if he thinks it's horrible or unnatural or some other hateful thing? What if he doesn't accept it?"

I stare at the door hoping they come back soon, because if Em has to sit here thinking that Dad hates her she's going to lose it. And then my aunt is going to come up here and make things ten times worse.

A few minutes later they come back in. Dad has wiped the shocked look off his face and sits down next to Em.

"I'm sorry I didn't react better." He's silent for a minute while he searches for the words. "I . . . I'm afraid for you."

"What are you afraid of?"

"I love you so much," he says, nearly crying. "I'm afraid that your life is going to be harder because of who you are, and I'm not going to be able to protect you."

Em's whole expression changes. "I'll be fine. It's been fine. People at school don't care. Plenty of people don't care."

"Plenty still do, and I'm just scared that you're going to meet people who don't give you a chance because of who you love."

"That's no reason for me to hide."

"No. No, and I wouldn't want you to be anything other than who you are. I'm glad you told us. I just keep thinking about all the people who are against you for no reason, and I'm scared. You're looking at a terrified father. Not a father who doesn't love you, or a father who doesn't accept you. I'm afraid that your life will be harder and that I won't be able to help."

The only other time I saw Dad this shaken up was when Pete went to war. And he's afraid for Em. Not without good reason. I've seen some of the people who hate her just because she's gay. I go to school with them.

"I'm not scared, Dad. I can handle this. It doesn't matter what ignorant people think. I only care that the people I love are okay with it. Are you okay?"

"Of course I am," he says, bringing her into a hug.

"I just wish I could protect you from the people who won't understand."

"More and more people are with us every day. It really is changing."

Mom says, "So now that we know a bit more, tell us about your girlfriend. We can't wait to meet her."

We all sit there and talk for a bit while Em tells us about Jamie. Then instead of going to bed we stay up and watch whatever dumb movie is on TV. Just all of us together hanging out, for the first time in months.

The next day I hang out with Seth and Margaret again. All the strangeness is gone. I do my entire show for them and Margaret makes suggestions to improve it and Seth and I are totally back to normal. By Sunday it almost feels like I live here again. A part of me never wants to go back to Colorado. I could just stay on Seth's couch through high school. Everything is so good right now, I don't know how I'm going to go back and face everyone at school. And face Tess. And then it's time to get on a plane and head back home.

From Wednesday through Saturday I was missing Tess pretty badly. Now that it's time to go home I'm sort of dreading seeing her again.

On the airplane I open my bag and take out my magic books. Half the pages are dog-eared and have highlighter marks and my notes written in the margins.

I start practicing my hand moves for my routine, but then I see Tess's letter. I'm about to put it back in my bag, and then say *screw it*, and open the envelope.

Even though it's cold on the plane my body is sweating, making me hot and cold at the same time. I already know the worst it could say, so I don't know why I'm freaking out. *I hate you. I ruined my relationship with my family for a jerk like you. Never speak to me again.* I'm expecting all that and more. And I deserve it. That's the worst part.

I look to my left and make sure Dad is still sleeping, then start to read.

Dear Ben,

I'm sorry I can't say this to you in person. It's too hard right now. I care about you so much, but hearing you say what you did showed me that you don't respect my beliefs or me.

I've gone out of my way to try to make you feel welcome here and to be considerate of your beliefs. It seems obvious to me now that you haven't given my faith any respect at all. What you said hurt. Not just because it was hateful toward my religion, but also because it felt like you were attacking me.

James explained to me what made you so mad. How Mr. Thompson failed you and how Kenny tripped you. I'm sorry about your grade. I don't want to say I told you so, but this is what I was worried about. I'm not saying you deserved that grade. But no one within earshot of your rant deserved what you said either. Especially me.

I hope you understand why I can't be with you. It hurts me more than you know. I hope one day you'll be able to understand that even though other people don't think the same way as you, their opinions are just as important.

I miss you.

Tess

No *I hate you?* No *You're the worst person ever?* I want to rip her letter in two. Not because I'm angry but because I messed up. I mean, I came to Colorado being like, *where I come from everyone accepts each other's differences.* And it's true. For the most part. But I didn't. I came there and as soon as I felt people judge me for my beliefs I started to judge them right back. Including Tess.

I don't understand how anyone could believe in a god, but it makes sense to her, and that's what matters. Even before I yelled Jesus effing Christ, I wasn't being fair to her. I made fun of her in a way she never made fun of me. Even if I didn't say it, I was thinking it. And I treated her unfairly, from not trusting her to be cool about my sister, to bashing the Bible.

When the plane gets to the gate, I still feel like crap. With Tess avoiding me, it's not like I can just apologize. And because of me she won't get to go to her brother's wedding. It's because of me we're not together anymore.

We swing by James's house on the way home to check on him and his mom and to pick up Holly.

When we pull up, Holly is at the window. She nearly knocks James over when he opens the door to let us in.

"Dude, are you okay?" he asks when he sees my face.

"I read the letter," I whisper.

"Oh."

"Yeah."

"How are you doing?" my mom says loudly as she walks in. "We missed you so much!" She gives him a big hug, nearly squeezing the air out of him. "How was your Thanksgiving?"

"It was good, thanks. My mom is sleeping right now. She's doing really great. She's just taking it slow."

"I'm so glad to hear it. If you need anything," she says, "anything at all, either of you, just say the word and we'll be here."

"Thanks," says James. "I think Holly helped her a lot too. She slept in her bed and sat with her a lot."

"She's a good girl," says my mom, as she rubs Holly's ears. "You took good care of her and we appreciate it."

Holly just keeps circling around our legs to show how excited she is to have everyone here.

"You want to hang out for a bit?" asks James.

"Nah, I should get home. I've got some stuff I have to figure out."

"Okay. I'll see you tomorrow."

My mom hugs James as we head out. Holly jumps in the back seat and immediately lays her front paws and chin over my legs.

Chapter 37

OLDER BROTHERS ARE SMARTER THAN YOU

On Monday I go back to school with a new plan. I've got three weeks left here. Only two weeks left to get back in the talent show and one week more to get Tess to forgive me. Even if she doesn't want to be with me. I just want her to know how sorry I am. She said in her letter that she missed me. Maybe that's still true. Maybe that will be enough for her to hear me out.

It feels like getting back into the talent show and getting Tess not to hate me are tied together. Like, if I can do one, I can do the other.

Over the next few days I leave three notes in Tess's locker saying I really need to talk to her. Nothing. Not a word back.

She just hangs with Beth, who does look at me. More with pity than anything else. Tess just pretends I don't exist.

On Thursday, Pete comes home, which gets me out of my sad, self-pitying state of mind. It's about 4 o'clock and Dad is making Pete's favorite dinner of stuffed shells and Mom is hanging up a banner that says "Welcome Home" on the front door. Pete shows up in his uniform with short hair and a massive backpack in his hand. He looks older. Further away.

Mom runs up and hugs him. He drops his pack and hugs her back, a tired smile on his face. Then Dad. Then me. And then, the girl he really missed more than any of us. Holly. She's wiggling around on the ground like an eel out of water. One second she's licking his face, the next she's on her back, and then she's running in circles around him.

Pete's the one who picked Holly out at the pound. The pound only had a three-day hold for dogs without tags. She was going to be killed later that day. He saved her life. Not that she knows that.

He gets down on the ground and lies flat on his back while Holly jumps all over him and licks his face. Then he goes to his room, puts his stuff down, and gets in the shower. He stays in there for like twenty minutes. When he comes downstairs, he's in his jeans and a T-shirt.

We all sit down to dinner. Everyone is quiet. Not in a weird way. Pete is always kind of distant his first few days back. I mean, I can't imagine what it's like going from a war zone where bombs are going off and people you know can die, to suburbia where the biggest problems are ones like mine. My ex-girlfriend won't talk to me. Sounds kind of stupid when I think of it like that.

After dinner and dessert, Pete heads upstairs and goes to bed. It's still early but he looks exhausted. He takes Holly outside one last time and then he takes her upstairs to his room. Holly sleeps in my room most of the time, but it's understood that I'm second best. When Pete gets home she barely leaves his side.

That night I set my alarm for 4 a.m. It's nine hours ahead in Iraq, so whenever Pete comes home he goes to sleep early, then wakes up in the middle of the night and watches movies.

When I get down to the den, he's already there with a bowl of cereal and Holly on his lap.

"Hey," he says, turning off the television. "You look good. Older."

"You too," I say.

He takes a bite of his cereal.

"You have school today?" he asks.

"Yeah. The semester is almost over. Then I'm out of there."

"Mom told me. You're lucky. None of us ever got to go to public school."

"Lucky isn't what I'd call it. You've never been to a really religious school."

He just shakes his head and says, "It's amazing how pretty much every religion preaches peace, but most of them can't manage to live up to it, huh?"

"The Buddhists?" I ask. "The Dalai Lama doesn't really throw down."

"I guess not."

"Plus, there are lots of people who believe in all the stuff religion cares about, and do it right. Peace and good deeds and loving thy neighbor. It's like the few bad kids making the whole class seem like it's out of control."

"Look at you. Coming to the defense of religion."

"I'm just saying, people are messed up no matter what they believe. We always find a reason to hate each other. There is good too. There wouldn't be any point if there wasn't."

"In a war you don't really get to see the good stuff," he says glumly and turns back to his cereal.

"What happened to that dog you were taking care of?"

"They wouldn't let me bring her home but my friend Gary is taking care of her."

"Still want to open up a shelter?"

"I'm thinking about it. I have one more tour, then I'm out. I have to do something."

He gets all quiet for a minute or two while he pets Holly's face. Her eyes are closed. All of a sudden, Pete remembers that I'm here and looks at me.

"How are things going with your girl?" he asks.

"They aren't. She broke up with me."

"Because you got suspended?"

"Because of what I said that got me suspended."

"That sucks."

"She was right. It was my fault."

"Your teacher treated you like hell from what Mom said."

"Doesn't mean I get to act like a jerk."

"True," he says. "Does that mean we aren't going to her brother's wedding?"

"Looks like it."

"Why isn't she going with her parents?"

"Her brother is an atheist so they don't speak to him."

"Seriously? So she's not going now? That's bull. You can't let that happen."

"She won't even talk to me. I doubt she'll let me be her date for the wedding."

"Imagine if I were getting married and you and Em weren't there," he says. "It's his wedding."

"What should I do?"

"When is it again?"

"The day after the talent show. December fourteenth."

"We're going. Tess is going. You've just got to make it happen."

"She won't even look at me."

"Then make it up to her. You messed up, so it's up to you to fix it."

"I don't know how. I've been thinking about it, but I seriously have no idea how to get her to listen to me."

"You better think of something," he grins at me.

"Thanks," I say, sarcastically. "You want to watch a movie?"

"Show me the best thing I've missed since I've been gone."

"You got it."

"Then you can show me this routine you've got going on at the talent show. I've got to make sure you're not going to embarrass yourself."

That day at school I basically stalk Beth until I find her at her locker during a free period. I come up to her as she's getting some books out.

"Hey, Beth. Can I talk to you?"

"Not without Tess getting mad at me."

"Tess doesn't need to know."

"I don't keep secrets from my best friend," she says.

"She kept one from you. Consider this payback."

She kind of shakes her head and turns back to her locker.

"This is for Tess," I say. "Come on. It's important."

She turns back around and looks at her watch. "You have two minutes. Tess is waiting for me in the library."

"Ask her to hang out on the day her brother is getting married. Just make sure she has an excuse to be out of her house."

"She's not going to the wedding, Ben. She can't. She has no way to get there."

"She might. I'm working on something but I can't tell her. Just please play along. Ask her to a movie or the mall or something. If I can't come through or if she doesn't want to go because she hates me too much, then you'll still have movie plans."

She looks at me with that disapproving face she's so good at making.

"Please?" I beg.

"Fine, but you better not mess with her. She's devastated that she can't go."

"Leave it to me."

Chapter 38

MIDNIGHT PHONE CALLS

F ive days before the talent show, James calls my cell at like midnight. I'm sound asleep so when I answer, I don't even think. I just say, "Is your mom okay?"

"Yeah. It's not about that. It's Kenny's brother, the one in Iraq. He died."

"What? When?"

"His family was just told tonight. I was at church with my mom and they were all there. I thought you'd want to know."

"Yeah. Thanks."

"Okay. Well, I'll let you get back to sleep."

I hang up, but instead of going back to sleep I just lay there. I don't even have thoughts. Just a physical reaction. My heart is racing and I'm sweating. Pete just got home and he's safe, but he has to go back.

I wonder what happened to Kenny's brother. Maybe Pete knew him. Probably not, but maybe. I get out of bed and my heart slows a bit. My shirt is still wet with sweat. I walk down the hall to Pete's room and open the door. He's not there. I find him downstairs, just sitting in the dark looking out the window with Holly at his feet.

"You okay?" I ask.

"Couldn't sleep."

"James just called," I say. "One of the kids in my school, the one who's been messing with me, his brother died. He was in Iraq."

Pete doesn't say anything. He just nods. After a minute or two he asks, "What's his last name?"

"Schrock. I don't know his first name."

"I don't know any Schrocks."

"Kenny doesn't like me, and I just might hate him, but I'm not sure that matters. I thought, if you want to, we could go to the funeral together."

"We should." Pete looks at the clock on the wall and says, "It's late. You should go to bed."

"You too?"

"Not tired."

"Okay," I say, trying to figure out if I should go back to bed or just sit in silence with him. He doesn't look back my way. "Night."

I head upstairs to my room. Pete always sounds normal in his emails to me from wherever he's stationed. When he gets home he's just so quiet. I mean, this happens every time he comes home. Usually after a few days he gets into the swing of things and starts sleeping full nights. Then he starts joking around again, being more like his old self. It seems harder for him this time. Like he doesn't fit here.

Kenny is surrounded by people at school over the next few days. A special assembly is even called to talk about our war heroes and how great they are, even when it costs them and their families so much.

I don't go up to Kenny to say anything. I don't want to get in his way. He might punch me just for talking to him. Jerk or not, he lost his brother. We may not believe the same things, but we both had brothers in the service, and that means something.

The talent show is in a few days and I know I should be practicing, or figuring out a way to get back in it. Maybe beg Trent to sneak me onstage or something. Instead, I'm finding it hard to concentrate on anything, even my homework, and I have finals next week. I'm so close to being done with this school for good and all I can think about is Kenny and Pete. Pete is only back here for a month and then he has to go back to Iraq. His next tour will be longer.

Instead of doing the stuff I'm supposed to do, I watch movies with Pete. He's barely left the house since he got back. Not that he knows anyone here to hang out with. So we sit together with snacks my dad makes us and put in DVDs. Ones that we've seen already, but it doesn't matter. We watch and we laugh and we don't talk. Not about anything that matters anyway.

On Wednesday afternoon, two days before the talent show, Pete takes James and me to the funeral. He hadn't touched his uniform since he got back. It just sat in a crumpled pile in the corner of his room, until this morning, when he washed it and broke out the iron to make it perfect.

There are a bunch of guys in uniform already at the funeral when we arrive. And pretty much the entire school. Pete nods at the men and women in uniform.

They nod back, but he stays with me. Tess is up front sitting with her family. She hasn't seen me yet. The place is packed.

Pete, James, and I walk up to the front to pay our respects. There is no place to kneel like at the other funerals I've been to. So we just sort of stand in front of him for thirty seconds or so.

I do what I did at my grandmother's funeral a few years ago; I stare at the lining of the casket. That way it looks like I'm looking at the dead person. Really I'm avoiding it. What I can't avoid is seeing that he's in uniform. The same uniform my brother is wearing. And that brings my eyes up to his face. I've only ever seen old people like this. Dead. He's got to be nineteen or twenty.

Without meaning to, my eyes get wet. I hold them open to try to dry them out, but tears are building up above my lower lid.

Pete looks over at me, sees my face, and puts his hand on my shoulder. That does it. The tears drop and I'm officially crying. Not big sobs or anything. Just face- burning kind of tears.

Pete could die.

Pete moves me away from the coffin. James follows us. I see Kenny sitting with his family. I walk up to him and say, "I'm sorry." I'm looking him straight in the eye, something I'd never do at school. I need him to know I get it. He's not alone.

He sees my face and I can tell he knows that any more words out of me would be followed by more tears.

"Thanks," he says and nods at my brother. His family gives us all sad nods and then we move toward the back of the church.

I feel Tess looking at me. For the first time I don't try to make eye contact. Today isn't about her. It's about this guy who died. Sean.

We get to our seats, way in the back, and look around. At the front of the church on a big screen is a slideshow showing pictures of Kenny's brother, Sean. From him as a kid to what could have been last spring.

While we wait for the service to start a bunch of people come up to Pete to say thanks for his service and for keeping us safe. Pete nods back, but doesn't really talk to anyone.

Finally the funeral starts. It seems like the pastor really knew Sean. He tells stories about him and his family from years ago. He talks about how Sean played football in high school and loved to play guitar. About how he performed at the church a whole bunch and how he loved his country. Sean had been offered a scholarship to go to college. He didn't go. He felt his place was protecting people so he enlisted.

Pete stays motionless through the entire thing. No tears, no nothing. Just a blank face as he listens to the pastor.

Once the pastor stops talking about Sean as a man, he talks about everlasting peace, and says that because Sean was a Christian, he's in heaven with god right now.

I watch Kenny, or at least the back of his head. He's not looking at the pastor. He's looking down. His mom's arm is around his shoulder.

I stop listening and just think about my brother next to me. This is why he's up at night. He has seen people he knew die. Guys who are so young, they might still be virgins, or they've never owned a car. Or maybe the war was their first trip out of the country. Pete must think about dying. About who would miss him. Would he have as many people at his funeral as Sean?

I feel freaking miserable. It gets so bad that I'm sweating again. Like Pete is dead already and I can't stop my mind from thinking about it. Like this is his funeral. I see my mom and dad and sister crying. His best friends from high school. His old teachers like his history teacher who thought he was the best student he ever had. Lots of people to miss him and to feel like the world was changed because of his loss.

As soon as the service is over I get up and go to the bathroom. Standing and walking makes me feel better. I've got to get myself together.

When I get to the bathroom and open the door I see Kenny standing at the counter looking in the mirror. He's been crying.

He sees me, and he starts all over again, his shoulders shaking.

I just stand there with the door half open and look at the ground.

"If you're coming in, come in," he says, between breaths.

I let the door close, but I don't move any closer.

"You know only around four thousand soldiers have died in this war. Two million troops deployed in Iraq and Afghanistan since 9/11 and only four thousand deaths. That's nothing. Absolutely nothing."

He looks at me, forcing me to raise my eyes up to his.

"In World War Two," he says, "over four hundred thousand Americans died. You don't expect people to come home with numbers like those. It's just a bonus if they do. But less than four thousand? Those are good odds."

"I'm sorry," I say, which is totally useless. His brother is dead and mine isn't. He wipes his eyes with his sleeve, looks away from me, and says, "So you really don't believe in God? Well, what the hell happens to people in your world if there is no God?"

His face scrunches up and he looks completely deflated, like he's lost everything that will ever matter to him.

"It doesn't matter what I believe," I say, finally. "Who says I'm right about anything?"

"Then no one says I'm right either."

I step toward him. "You believe in god. You believe your brother is in heaven. So that's where he is."

"If your brother died," he says, looking at me straight in the eye, "where do you think he'd go?"

I think to myself, *in the ground*, but what worse thing could you possibly say to someone who just lost their brother. For the first time I see why it matters, why heaven is so damn important. No one ever really leaves you. Not forever. Death doesn't rip a person from your life, it just means you have to wait to see them again. So I say, "All that matters is what you think. Your brother, he was saved, right?"

"Yeah."

"Then you know exactly where he is."

He breathes in deeply and turns on the tap to splash water on his face.

"Does your brother have to go back?" he asks, drying his face.

"Yeah."

"The odds are on his side," he says, not even looking at me. Kenny throws the paper towel in the garbage and walks past me. As he opens the door to leave he stops, turns his head, and says, "I'm sorry I tripped you. That was messed up." Then he's gone.

I splash some cold water on my face to stop the stinging in my eyes. For the rest of his life, Kenny will have to live with his brother being dead. I still have Pete, and suddenly I feel like the luckiest kid in the world.

I walk back out to the main room where people are still standing around talking to each other. There are hundreds of people and they all look comforted. Like they know that Sean is still out there, that they'll see him again.

I can see why that would be something to hold on to and why Kenny needs that to be true. Everyone here *knows* that they will live forever, even if it's not on earth.

I feel like I understand why someone would want to believe in something bigger. How scary it must be to go from believing you live forever in heaven to believing you die and you're gone.

I don't mind the idea of being gone forever. It makes life more important somehow. What I do right now matters because it's all I have. But believing in something bigger helps people deal. I bet it even makes it easier to be willing to die for your country.

I look at Pete and wonder if he's ever believed, even just for a second when he's scared. Or if he's ever hoped that he's wrong. That there is a god.

I get now why my freak-out at school hurt everyone so badly. Jesus is the guy who takes care of them in situations like these. That's a big freaking deal. And I completely disrespected their savior. I have to say sorry to everyone. Up until now it's felt like Tess is the only person I hurt. Really, I've hurt the entire school, and I have to do something to fix it.

Pete, James, and I get up to walk out to the parking lot. The aisle is so crowded I just try not to bump into other people. When we're almost to the door I feel someone grab my hand, give it a fast squeeze, and then let go.

Tess rushes by me with a quick look back over her shoulder.

I don't even have time to smile or nod or anything before she's facing forward again and speed walking ahead to catch up with her family. I can feel her hand on mine still, that warm skin and pressure, even though it was for less than a second. I can feel her.

After the funeral we drop James off and head back to the house.

Pete is still quiet. He's barely said a word since we got in the car to go to the funeral. Once James leaves and we're alone, it kind of feels like Pete wants to say something. We get all the way home and pull into the driveway and still he hasn't said a word. But he doesn't get out of the car.

So I sit there too, not speaking, just looking at my knees.

After a few minutes Pete finally says, "That was my first one."

"First what?" I ask.

"First army funeral."

I don't say anything.

"I've lost friends over there, and we have a drink in their name, but their body gets sent back here and we never get to go."

"I'm sorry," I say, not knowing what else I could say.

"I don't want to go back."

I nod.

"One more tour. Then I'm out."

"Then you'll start that shelter."

"Damn right."

"Maybe you could start raising money for it now," I say.

"I should do that," Pete says.

"There's one near here. We could go and walk some dogs."

He looks at me for the first time.

"That would be great," he says.

"I stopped eating meat over Thanksgiving break. I mean, what the hell is the difference between a dog and a pig anyway?"

"Emily finally got to you?"

"Her friend Ed. He made a good point. There is no difference. An animal is an animal."

"Death is death," says Pete.

I turn and face him. "I'm glad you're home."

"You figure out a way to get Tess to the wedding on Saturday?" he asks.

"I think I might have. It depends."

"On what?"

"On whether or not she'll forgive me."

Chapter 39

TAKING OUT YOUR STOPPED HEART AND HANDING IT TO THE PEOPLE WHO HATE YOU

At school on Friday the teachers let anyone in the talent show out of second period to practice for tonight. A full dress rehearsal. Admission is ten bucks a person. We're hoping that parents open up their wallets and give more.

It's my last day to make something happen and get back in the show. My tricks are solid. I might even get an 'oooh' or an 'ahhhh' if I can get onstage.

The school assembly is at the end of the day today. I have one shot to ask for forgiveness and hope that gets me back into the show.

I want to leave this school letting everyone know that atheists aren't terrible people, that I'm sorry for saying what I said, and that if we all try really hard we can be nice to each other.

Tess passes me in the hall without saying a word. Yesterday at the funeral was just a one-time thing I guess. Maybe she felt bad for me. Now it's back to no eye contact.

I keep thinking of that hand squeeze. Of her taking the time and risk to separate from her family and loop back around just to give me that small sign.

I'm walking from English to lunch up in the library when I pass Kenny and he gives me a nod and says, "Hey."

"Hey," I say back in surprise.

That's the entire conversation, but suddenly I feel like it can happen. Like I can do this.

I spend lunchtime practicing my routine for James. I'm able to do it two and a half times through without a problem. At this point, it's not even the show that I'm nervous about. It's what I'm going to do during the assembly that has me freaked out. The thing I'll do if I'm brave enough, if I don't get so scared that I flake out.

Everyone at this school has treated me like crap. The thing is, I haven't treated them much better. They deserve something from me. Something other than the condescending attitude of a judgmental jerk.

I think about what I want to say to everyone. It changes each time. Maybe a simple *I didn't mean to say what I said* or *I was really upset*. Maybe just, *I'm sorry but don't worry, I'm leaving this hellhole soon so we don't have to see each other anymore.*

I get through the rest of my classes, barely paying attention. James meets me at my locker to walk over to the assembly. Frank starts it off by talking again about god and being saved. It's like watching one episode of the only show on TV on repeat.

I started tuning it out after the third assembly. This week I'm listening closely. Waiting for Frank to ask the question 'has anyone been saved?'

Technically my answer is no. I'm still not saved and probably never will be, but I need the mic. We get past the end-of-year stuff, the plug for the talent show tonight, and then Frank says it.

"Would anyone like to come up here to share their story? It's December. The end of one year with a new one beginning. Wouldn't it feel great to start by knowing that if the Lord took you tomorrow, you know where you'd be headed?"

It takes me a second to get my legs to work. I'm trying to stand up. It's just not happening. I look over at James, my eyes wide and freaked out, so he does what any good friend would do. He takes his pencil and he jabs it into my leg. Not hard enough to break skin Just hard enough so that my eyes water and I stand up.

"Me. I have something to say."

Frank hesitates and looks a little concerned, but no kid is denied the stage. Not when it's about the soul.

I walk down to the stage rubbing my leg where James stabbed me. Each kid is staring at me, looking kind of pissed. A couple of them laugh nervously. One or two chimp noises come from the back. Frank puts his finger to his lips and everyone quiets down.

Now it's silent.

Frank gives me a look as he hands me the microphone, like he's trying to figure out if I'm going to start screaming at everyone from stage. I nod at him, trying to let him know he can trust me.

Damn. I'm really going to do this. Hundreds of eyes bore into me and I clear my throat nervously.

"I know people usually come up here to tell the story of how they got saved. I don't have a story like that, but I do have something that I need to say."

I see Tess a few rows back. She's looking at me like she's waiting at the dentist for a root canal.

"About a month ago, I said something at school that hurt a lot of people. I'm not a bad person," I say. "But what I said, even though I was mad when I said it, wasn't okay. It was a cheap shot. It was wrong of me. It was mean and disrespectful and I'm sorry."

I look at Tess as I say this. She's staring at me with her mouth open.

"I'm going to a public school starting in January so you won't be seeing me in school anymore. Which is probably better for everyone. I've learned a lot by being here. I think I've learned how to be more respectful of people whose beliefs I don't really understand. I know what it's like to be made fun of for being different. I hope none of you ever have to feel that.

"Anyway, you should all go to the talent show tonight. It's to raise money for sick kids. Plus the acts are pretty great."

I hand the mic back to Frank. The auditorium is silent. Not that I thought I was going to get a standing ovation or anything. I had hoped for some acknowledgment. I turn to walk off stage when I hear clapping. I look over and it's Tess and Beth, both putting their hands together like they were at a concert.

For a solid five seconds it's just them and they look like maniacs. Then the rest of the school jumps in. Not as enthusiastically but it's not pathetic either. It's a *we forgive you sort of but we still don't like you* clap. Which is better than what I was working with before.

I go backstage and wait for Frank. He wraps up the assembly, looking over at me a few times, then dismisses everyone and walks toward me.

"That was a good thing you just did. Apologizing to everyone like that."

"They deserved an apology."

He looks at me without saying anything, just waiting.

"I wanted to ask," I say, stopping and feeling nervous. If he says no, I'm done. No show. All that hard work for nothing. "I want back in the talent show. I worked hard to put my act together and I want to be there to help raise money for those kids. I know what I did was wrong. And I was punished for it, in more ways than just getting suspended. So I'm asking. Please let me perform tonight. You can trust me."

Frank looks at me for a long time, like he's trying to read my mind. I don't look away. I don't back down. I want this.

"Okay," he says finally. "You're back in."

Chapter 40

THE TALENT SHOW

At six o'clock, when Pete drives me back to school I feel like a new man. The school year is over and I'm going to start fresh in a new place. Tess clapped, which means she doesn't hate me. I've got my routine totally down for tonight. It's one of those rare times that life as a teenager doesn't totally blow.

When we pull up in front of the school Tess is sitting on a bench outside. She sees our car and stands.

"Um."

"What?" asks Pete, stopping the car.

"That's Tess."

"Then you should get out of the car and go talk to her."

"It's daylight and in public."

"Stop being such an ass and go talk to her. She's clearly waiting for you."

When I still don't move, Pete undoes my seatbelt, reaches across me, opens the door, and pushes me out of the car. His military reflexes must be top-notch because he seemed to do all that in one motion.

I stumble out of the car and Tess looks at me, not smiling or scowling. Just sort of staring and waiting. Before I even open my mouth to say "hey," Pete is walking up to Tess with his hand out.

"I'm Pete," he says.

"Ben told me a lot about you," Tess says.

"Dude," I say, walking up to them.

"Oh, sorry. I thought you were just going to keep standing there. Tess, it was nice to meet you. Ben, break a leg tonight."

Pete heads into the school with a magazine.

"Hey," I say to Tess.

"Hi."

"Do you want to go inside?" I ask. "We're kind of out in the open."

"Just sit," she says, pointing to the bench behind her.

We sit down. Not too close to each other.

"I loved what you said today," says Tess. "It was pretty brave going up there."

"I wanted to do it before I left, you know?"

"Yeah. It was a weird way to find out that you're transferring."

"Sorry."

"I think you'll be happier someplace else. I'm kind of jealous, actually."

"You'd want to go to public school?"

"I'd like to know what it's like to be around people who aren't all the same. I mean, I've never done much of anything outside of my family. One day I want to do things on my own, like go to Europe or Asia. Anywhere really. Maybe I'll join the Peace Corps."

"It's just public school. It's not like it's public school in Italy. Although that would be awesome."

"You know what I mean. I've really liked hanging out with people who weren't brought up the same way I was, who challenged me to learn new things."

"Yeah."

"I should get inside and check all the props."

"Tess?"

"Yeah?"

"I'm sorry. I know I said it to everyone, and that included you, but I need to say it to you personally. It was stupid and wrong and I was a total jerk."

"Thanks, Ben."

She puts her hand over mine for just a second and then gets up to go inside.

"I miss you too," I say. "You know, just in case you were wondering."

She smiles and moves her hair out of her face and says, "Good luck tonight."

I follow Tess inside the auditorium and Trent sees me and says, "Welcome back. We're all glad you're here."

"Thanks, man."

Trent gets us all organized and gives a speech about how great we're going to be and how all our hard work is going to pay off. He says we're expecting four hundred people in the audience tonight.

I feel like I should be nervous, but all I feel is happiness and relief. It's not like Tess jumped back into my arms and said *I can't live without you* or anything like that. She did talk to me. And she did it in public. Maybe she'll even consider being my friend. I could use another one.

It's weird being backstage. This is where Tess and I were sneaking around when we got caught. It was so quiet when it was just us and now all the talent show kids are running around getting ready. One kid is puking in the bathroom.

I get myself together and make sure all my stuff is ready to go before the first act goes onstage. Then, I sit and listen.

We've got music. We've got drama. From backstage it sounds like everyone is doing a great job. Trent is kicking it as a host and reminding the crowd that they are all here to help the kids at the hospital, so give what you can.

I'm the last act. For the first few performances I just kind of sat back and listened. Now we're in the second half of the show and I'm feeling my gut start to move around. In a good way though, like right before my first kiss with Tess.

Maybe at my next school I'll get students together to do a show with me to raise money for Pete's shelter. That way when he gets back from his next tour he'll have some money to get started.

The final act before mine is onstage singing some Christian song. The audience loves it, which is good. There'll be high energy when I get out there.

My stomach is turning, like the earth might be rotating inside my gut.

Next thing I know Tess is grabbing my arm and pulling me toward the stage.

"Are you deaf? It's your turn! Are you ready?"

I look at the stage, trying to see what the auditorium looks like when it's packed with people.

"I guess it doesn't matter," says Tess, when I don't respond. "You're on."

I barely have time to think about how scared I am

now that the time is actually here. I've got a job to do. Entertain. Be a freaking awesome magician.

I walk onstage with a big smile, stand behind the table, and grab my first prop. The egg illusion. A great starter.

I go through all the illusions knowing that the amount of applause I get at the end will tell me two things. How good my performance was. And how good my apology was. If they forgive me or not. I bet every person in this room heard about what I said. And I hurt them all.

As I break into the big part of my set, the card manipulations, I feel more nervous than I did before I even went on. I start with the easier stuff, fanning, and then I keep upping it. Harder and harder. My fingers are moving fast and have to be just right. I look at the audience as well as at my hands. A great magician can't just have the moves down, they need to connect with the audience. To be so confident that the movement of the cards looks effortless. And I'm doing it. I'm making the sleights of hand that Margaret helped me with, and my fingers are moving over the cards so easily that McBride himself would be proud. I'm a freaking magician.

I do the last set of card moves, close the deck into my palm, smile, and bow. What starts as a few claps turns into a few more. I bow again to indicate that the show is over and then the whole crowd starts clapping. Well, almost everyone. A few families sit totally still, not moving. But Kenny, Arty, and Beth are all clapping and smiling at me.

I look offstage to see Tess clapping too. Her eyes are shiny and wet looking. A few seconds later all the kids come out and join me for our final bows. Tess is the first onstage and takes my hand. She squeezes it tight and although she doesn't look at me I can see her crying.

The crowd keeps clapping until Trent steps forward.

"Thank you all for coming," he says. "I've just been told that the count for the night is five thousand six-hundred and twenty-two dollars! That's how much we raised to help the kids at the hospital. We'll be doing the same show for them tomorrow and give them the check. Thank you all for coming and God bless."

We walk offstage together. As soon as we're all backstage, people start hugging and congratulating each other. Even me.

Tess comes up from behind and gives me a huge hug.

"You were sooooo good," she says. "Seriously, they loved you."

"You're talking to me. Again." I say. "Aren't you afraid people will see?"

"Did you hear me? You were great!"

"What's the deal? We spend the whole semester pretending we don't know each other and now you're talking to me in public twice in one night."

"You were really brave today saying what you did in front of all those people. You've been brave this entire time and you've stayed true to who you are. I've decided to do the same, so I'll talk to who I want to. I'm not hurting anyone. I'm not doing anything bad. If someone wants to tell on me, and my parents want to ground me, then that's their choice. I'm done hiding."

"Can you hide for one more day?"

"Huh?"

"Well, you know how you're going to the mall with Beth tomorrow?"

"How did you know that?"

"I asked her to make those plans so that we could all go to your brother's wedding."

She goes from looking shocked to looking like she just won the lottery.

"Are you kidding?! I'm going to the wedding?!"

"We all are."

Tess starts to cry. The kind of crying that looks odd because it's on the happiest face I've ever seen in my life.

"I can't believe you! I need to sit down."

"If you tell the truth tonight they might stop you."

"Okay. One more day of lying. Then that's it."

Chapter 41

TALENT SHOW TAKE TWO

When we all get to the hospital the kids are already waiting for us in the large common room. Some kids are sitting with IV's stuck in their arms. Some kids were rolled in the room in their beds. Others hardly look sick, except for their bald heads.

When we walk in the room each kid smiles and looks at us like we're the coolest people ever. There are probably only twenty kids in the room, but it feels so much more important than what we did last night.

While the first group sets up, I go around the room and introduce myself to each kid. Then Tess and everyone else goes around and introduces themselves, careful not to shake hands or anything in case we're carrying germs.

David, Elizabeth, Meredith, Alex, Mark, Lori, Brad, Molly, Jacob, Renee, Jane, Dan, Rachael, Darren, Doug, Jessica, Audrey, Sunny, Kim, and Stephanie. That's our audience. That's who we have to impress.

And we do a great job. For the next hour the kids smile, laugh, and clap. They sing along with the songs.

A few of them sneak up real close to my table when I'm doing my card manipulations. They give the "oohs" and "ahhs" that I hoped for.

Trent presents the hospital with the check. He also takes out a special surprise, something we didn't even know about. It's a box of toys for their playroom with board games and stuffed animals and action figures.

Before we leave, the kids give us each a thank-you card decorated by one of them.

If I hadn't been here, I wouldn't have been a part of this. I wouldn't have given these kids a great day. I look at Tess and she smiles at me. A genuine smile, almost like when we were together.

We get on the bus and head back to school. James and Beth are there waiting for us. So is Pete. We all go into the bathroom and change into our wedding clothes. James and me in dress shirts and nice pants and the girls in dresses. Even Pete is dressed up in his suit. Two weeks after getting back, his hair is starting to grow longer than the peach fuzz it was when he first got home. He won't cut it until the day before he leaves again.

James and I are ready and go outside to meet Pete. We all turn around as the girls walk over to join us. Tess is dressed up in a bright blue strapless dress. She looks incredible.

She goes right up to Pete and says, "Thank you so much for taking us. You have no idea how much this means to me."

"I have every idea how much it means to you. Ben told me."

Tess turns to me and gives me a hug. Not a friend

hug either, she's pressed up against me and her cheek is against my cheek. She feels amazing.

"I miss you so much," I say. I can't help it, it just comes out.

"I miss you too," she says, as she lets go of me.

"Come on guys. We've got a two-hour drive ahead," says Pete. "James, you're up front with me. I need a navigation man."

James climbs in the passenger seat and Beth and I each take a window with Tess in the middle. We're touching. We can't not touch. When I try to scoot toward the door it just makes it more obvious that it can't be stopped. I'm sweating so hard I feel like I'm going to turn my shirt to soup.

"Did you tell your brother we're coming?" I ask, trying to be cool.

"No," says Tess. "He's going to flip."

"In a good way though, right?"

"A very good way."

"Do your parents know he's getting married?" asks James.

"I don't know. I couldn't act like I knew because I'm not supposed to talk to him. And they never mention him so even if they did know I think they'd pretend they didn't."

"Your brother didn't tell you?" asks Beth.

"I try not to talk to him about my parents. It's too hard for him."

"If he's an atheist then he's not getting married in a church, right? It's got to be strange," says Beth.

"What?" I ask.

"Being an atheist."

"You realize that you're in the car with three of us," I say. "You're outnumbered."

Beth turns white.

"Try not to think about it," says Tess. "What your parents don't know won't hurt them."

"They would kill me."

"That doesn't seem like the Christian thing to do," I say, smirking.

"Don't you think you've gotten in enough trouble for mocking religion?" says Tess sharply.

My stomach tightens. "Yes."

"That's what I thought," she says, smiling. "It's not so easy for some of us who aren't allowed to hang out with whoever we want."

"Don't worry, Beth, they won't find out you're here," I say, and turn to face Tess. "You know though, nothing has been easy for me since I moved here. I was the one up there apologizing, but at that school I was ignored, harassed and treated like crap pretty much every single day. No one even gave me a chance. I was immediately judged."

Tess starts to talk. I cut her off. "I'm not saying that what I did wasn't terrible. It was and I know it. But your parents, Mr. Thompson, and the kids at school, they were horrible to me. And I've never gotten an apology for that."

"You're not going to," says Beth. "Not that I don't think you deserve one."

"I guess I don't need one anymore. I'll be out of there soon enough."

"I can't believe you're really going," says Tess. "Just when I'm done caring if people see us together."

"He's just changing schools," Pete says. "It's not like he's moving across the country. You guys can get back together. Ben being at a different school might even make it easier."

The car goes silent. Pete opens his mouth for the first time in the car ride and that's what he says! He just put it out there and now, because there's such a deafening silence in the car, I can hear the sweat dripping down my back. What do I say now?

"I'd like that," says Tess, finally.

"You would?" I ask.

"Yeah. You're right, most of the school was awful to you. And while what you did was awful too, I know you feel bad about it."

I want to kiss her. Then I see Beth, James, and even Pete's eyes in the mirror staring at me. So I do the next best thing. I hug her.

Beth gives little claps and James holds up his hand to Pete for a high five.

"If that didn't work he would have killed you," says James to Pete.

"I can take him," Pete grins.

Beth and Tess spend the rest of the car ride trying to put on makeup while the car bounces around, which is pretty entertaining for the rest of us. Finally we arrive and jump out of the car. Tess looks super nervous and starts fanning herself with her purse.

"You okay?" I ask.

"I haven't seen him in over two years. It's just weird, you know?"

"He's going to be so happy to see you. And hopefully he won't mind a few party crashers."

Now that I'm standing in front of her, I can't resist anymore. I wrap my arms around her and kiss her. She puts her arms around my neck and pulls in closer.

Behind me, I hear James say to Beth, "Do you, uh, maybe want to go out some time? Go on a bike ride or something?"

"You're a freshman."

"So?"

"That's worse than being an atheist," she says.

"How about you give it a try? Be my date for the wedding, and if you hate it, that's it. Done."

Tess and I turn to watch James offer Beth his arm. She rolls her eyes and takes it.

"Come on, let's go inside," I say to everyone.

Chapter 42

THE ANSWER TO THE ULTIMATE QUESTION

We walk into the building and into an area set up kind of like how a church would be, but without any religious stuff, just flowers and lots of people sitting in rows waiting excitedly for the wedding to start.

Tess looks around but doesn't see anyone she knows.

She grabs my hand. "Come on. I want to go find my brother before it starts."

"We'll be back," I say to the group as Tess yanks me down the hall.

"Maybe upstairs," she says.

We go up the stairs hand in hand and poke our heads around a couple of open doors. Tess hears a deep voice from down the hall and stops dead in her tracks.

"Is that him?" I ask.

She lets go of my hand and walks softly over to the last door in the hall. She breathes deep and knocks.

"Yeah?" says a voice.

Tess waves me over to her and then opens the door. We walk in together.

I see a guy in a tux smiling the craziest, biggest smile I've ever seen in my entire life. He runs over, picks Tess up in the air, and hugs her, swinging her around in a circle.

Tess starts crying. Michael starts crying. It might be the happiest I've ever seen two people in my life.

I look behind Michael and my mouth opens in surprise. I see someone I wouldn't have thought I'd see here in a million years. Tess's mom.

I'm looking at her and she's looking at me like she's deciding whether or not she's allowed to be furious at Tess for being here and being with me.

Michael finally puts Tess down. He's talking a mile a minute, saying things like, "How did you get here? I can't believe you came. Look how big you got!"

Tess laughs and starts to answer, then she finally sees what I see. Her face goes white and it's like she forgot how to speak. She and her mom stare at the floor guiltily and everyone stands awkwardly silent for a minute while the two of them figure out who is going to speak first.

Finally Tess says, "I thought you were visiting Grandma today."

"I did visit," she says. "You were supposed to be with Beth at the mall."

"Beth is here. I, well, I couldn't miss Michael's wedding."

"Me, neither," she says.

"Does Dad know you're here?" asks Tess.

"No," says her mom. "He wouldn't understand."

"So you lied to him?"

Michael steps in and says, "I know neither of you expected to see each other here. And neither of you are really supposed to be here. But you are. And it's the best thing I could have hoped for." Tess and her mom both give him a smile.

Tess says, "Mom, you remember Ben." I smile nervously.

Mrs. Colston gives me a forced nod, then looks back at Tess and says, "I can understand you being here for your brother. But to be here with him? After we forbid you to see him? After what he said? That, I can't let pass."

"Mom, Ben is an atheist. Just like Michael. And Michael isn't a bad person. He's your son. Ben is a good person too, one of the best I know."

Tess's mom shakes her head, refusing to listen. "Michael has always been respectful of what we believe. This boy spat on the name of the Lord."

"He did. And he apologized for it in front of the entire school yesterday. What you're not seeing is that everyone in the school turned their backs on him because he was different. Everyone expected him to be more like us, but no one wanted to try and get to know him for who he really was.

"Mom," says Michael. "I know you worry that she'll be corrupted. That if your kids don't believe, they won't go to heaven. At some point you have to let us make our own choices."

"You have no idea how scared your father and I are for you, Michael," she says, almost crying.

"I know, Mom. I know."

There is a knock on the door. A man in a suit steps in and says, "It's time."

"Come on Tess, you're sitting with me," says her mom, holding her hand out.

Tess backs away and takes my arm.

"I came here with Ben. He's the one who helped me see my brother get married today and I'm sitting with him. You're welcome to join us."

Tess gives her brother one more huge hug. "Congratulations. I love you so much," she says with tears still in her eyes. She takes my hand and leads me out into the hallway and downstairs to the main room. James holds his hand up in the air and waves us over to the seats they saved for us.

We sit down and Tess remains absolutely still. She doesn't turn to see if her mom followed, she just squeezes my hand tightly.

"Are you okay?" I ask.

"I'm at my brother's wedding. I'm great."

"I know, but . . ."

"Let's worry about everything else later. I just want to celebrate."

"Okay."

"With you going to public school next year it might even be easier to sneak around. We won't have to pretend to ignore each other at school anymore."

I turn to James, Pete, and Beth to explain what just happened. They are all staring past me. I turn around to see what they're looking at. It's Mrs. Colsten, moving down the row and sitting next to her daughter.

James whispers to Pete, "Tess's mom."

Mrs. Colsten doesn't say anything. She's just sitting and looking forward like she's any other guest waiting for the ceremony to start.

Tess takes her mom's hand and then the music starts.

Michael and Cindy, his fiancé, do things a bit differently. They walk down the aisle together. No one gives anyone away.

It's probably the best ceremony I could think of. There's a Justice of the Peace who says some nice things about both of them and talks about the joy of marriage. Michael looks so happy up there. Tess and her mom are both crying next to me, hugging each other. Michael and Cindy kiss and everyone claps. That's what weddings do I guess. The big stuff makes you forget about the little stuff.

Everyone is clapping and the couple walks back down the aisle to the best part of any wedding. The food. Maybe Tess will make me dance. Once she finds out how bad I am, she'll wish she never got back together with me.

After all the food and the toasts and meeting a zillion different people, it comes time to go home. Michael walked around introducing us to all of his friends saying, "This is my sister and her boyfriend. Can you believe they're here!"

James, who is actually capable of dancing, spends the entire time on the dance floor with Beth, who seems to kind of like him.

Tess's mom stays away from us throughout the reception. Once everything is finishing up, she follows us out to the parking lot.

"I think I'm going to go home with my mom," says Tess. "We've got some stuff to talk about."

"You sure do," I say. "Including whether or not you're going to tell your dad that you were both here today."

"We're in it together. She can't throw me under the bus without outing herself. It's kind of perfect, actually."

"When will I see you?"

"I'm not hiding anymore. If they ground me you won't see me for a while, but they can't keep me grounded forever. So we'll make plans. Just like a normal couple."

"Talk to your mom about it," I say. "After today she might have some ideas of her own."

I go to kiss her but Tess shrinks back and gives a side-glance at her mom.

"I'm going to date you, but I'm not going to kiss you in front of my mom. That's just embarrassing."

"Got it."

Tess gives Pete, Beth, and James a hug and goes off with her mom who is doing her damndest to avoid eye contact with me.

"I'll sit in the back," says James as we make our way to the car.

Beth says, "Just because we danced doesn't mean we're going to do anything else."

"You had a good time. Don't even try to deny it. Now I'm going to sit in the back with you, and if you're lucky I might hold your hand."

"Are all atheists so arrogant?" She gives him a fake glare and he grins.

I look over at Pete who is smiling, I think for the first time since he got home. Not just a half sad grin. A real actual smile.

"What?" I ask.

"Nothing. It's just good to be home."

ACKNOWLEDGMENTS

To David and Glenda Berman, the very best parents in the whole world who always let me make my own choices.

To Gary Ploski, my partner, very best friend, and the most important person on this entire planet (to me).

To my agent, Laura Strachan, for her tireless effort, and her love of literature.

To everyone at Seven Stories Press for publishing work with a conscience.

To Anne Rumberger, a fantastic editor, and a champion for this book.

To the writing faculty at Sarah Lawrence College, including David Hollander, Brian Morton, Ernesto Mestre, Mary LaChapelle, Carolyn Ferrell, and Victoria Redel. I'm not sure where I'd be without any of you. Especially David who made me believe I could be a writer when I was just twenty years old.

To Renee Wicklund and Trent England, two incredible friends (and writers) who generously let me use their beliefs and experiences as research for the book, and who read and gave notes on early drafts.

To my cats, Magneto and Cthulhu, who slept on my legs/on my arms/on my laptop while I wrote this entire book.

To all the people out there who are bullied for being honest about who they are.

And to anyone out there who chooses to change the world through kindness.

ABOUT THE AUTHOR

ALI BERMAN is the author of *Choosing a Good Life: Lessons from People Who Have Found Their Place in the World*. She works as a humane educator for HEART, helping to educate kids about human rights, animal protection and environmental ethics. Ali was born in England, grew up in New York, and now lives and writes in Portland, Oregon, with her husband and two cats. *Misdirected* is her first novel.

ABOUT SEVEN STORIES PRESS

Seven Stories Press is an independent book publisher based in New York City. We publish works of the imagination by such writers as Nelson Algren, Russell Banks, Octavia E. Butler, Ani DiFranco, Assia Djebar, Ariel Dorfman, Coco Fusco, Barry Gifford, Martha Long, Luis Negrón, Hwang Sok-yong, Lee Stringer, and Kurt Vonnegut, to name a few, together with political titles by voices of conscience, including Subhankar Banerjee, the Boston Women's Health Collective, Noam Chomsky, Angela Y. Davis, Human Rights Watch, Derrick Jensen, Ralph Nader, Loretta Napoleoni, Gary Null, Greg Palast, Project Censored, Barbara Seaman, Alice Walker, Gary Webb, and Howard Zinn, among many others. Seven Stories Press believes publishers have a special responsibility to defend free speech and human rights, and to celebrate the gifts of the human imagination, wherever we can. In 2012 we launched Triangle Square *books for young readers* with strong social justice and narrative components, telling personal stories of courage and commitment. For additional information, visit www.sevenstories.com.